"A SERIOUS MISTAKE, STRANGER . . ."

There was a pounding of boot heels along the boardwalk out front and then a man came through the door, blocking most of the light. Long Rider had an immediate first impression of size, and then of anger; the man bearing down on them was even taller than Long Rider's six-foot-two, and his green eyes flashed with a wild gleam of rage. The clerk stepped back, but the big man had already reached the display case. He reached out across it with an arm like a tree branch. The clerk's small body flew into the air at the end of the arm, sailing into a corner of the store. The newcomer followed close behind, towering over the crumpled figure on the floor.

"Mr. Haywood!" the clerk cried. "Please, I beg you—"

The man named Haywood reached down and yanked the clerk to his feet. He cocked one huge fist, holding the clerk's collar in the other.

"Don't do it," Long Rider said.

"You're making a serious mistake," said Haywood.

"I'd be surprised," said Long Rider. "It's been more than ten years since I've made a mistake."

LONG RIDER

FAST DEATH

CLAY DAWSON

CHARTER BOOKS, NEW YORK

FAST DEATH

A Charter Book/published by arrangement with the author

PRINTING HISTORY
Charter edition/January 1989

ISBN: 1-55773-163-2

Charter Books are published by The Berkley Publishing Group,
200 Madison Avenue, New York, N.Y. 10016.
The name "CHARTER" and the "C" logo are trademarks belonging
to Charter Communications Inc.

10 9 8 7 6 5 4 3 2 1

FAST DEATH

CHAPTER ONE

The clerk was writing numbers in a ledger at the back of the store when something made him look up from the pages. His small hands jerked convulsively, almost upsetting the ink-stand. A man he had never seen before was leaning over a display case not more than ten feet away. The stranger was a big, hard-edged man who loomed even larger in a long animal hide coat. The coat was the main thing that kept the clerk's attention at first. It looked so heavy that it made him think of a knight in armor.

The clerk also thought the man sure as hell should have made some kind of noise coming into the store.

The stranger's head snapped up with the first hint of movement and the clerk found himself staring into a pair of pale grey eyes he would never forget. They were sharp, like a hawk's eyes, with the same absence of feeling or expression. It spooked the clerk to have someone looking at him that way, as if he didn't count for much in the world. The stranger kept staring at him and the clerk stood up, removing his spectacles with fingers that shook a little. He set the spectacles carefully on top of the ledger and slid around the side of his desk.

"Excuse me," he said with a nervous laugh. "I didn't hear you come in. You wearing moccasins or something?"

The customer glanced quizzically at his feet and the clerk looked down over the edge of the display case.

"Well I'll be damned," he said. "That's just what they are, aren't they?"

The stranger still didn't say anything and the silence stretched on for a moment while the clerk waited for some kind of reaction, maybe even a word of greeting. But the stranger continued to watch him in silence, his eyes without expression, and the clerk had a sudden feeling that these eyes would never show anything the stranger didn't want them to show.

They would, however, see things other people didn't want them to see.

"Well, of course I can see they're moccasins," said the clerk. "I just mean you don't . . . I mean, people don't wear 'em too much anymore. Maybe that's because there ain't too many squaws to *make* 'em anymore." He laughed again but it was a hollow sound in the silence that followed. The clerk was just noticing how dark the stranger's skin was. He hoped it was only the result of spending a lot of time in the sun and wind. "So tell me," he said, "are they comfortable?"

The stranger stared at him, still looking a little puzzled.

"Well, sure," the clerk said with another laugh. "Why else would you wear 'em, right? I mean, you wouldn't deliberately make yourself suffer." He didn't wait for an answer this time. He pulled a rifle out of the display case between them and caressed the barrel for a moment before he handed it across. "Anyway, I'll be this is what you were looking at. And well you might, my friend. It's the finest piece money can buy. Notice how good it feels in your—"

The clerk stopped short, gazing intently at the stranger's right hand. First he noticed the broken trigger finger, bent over sharply at the second joint. Then he saw the white puckered scar about halfway between the knuckles and the wrist. It looked even whiter against the stranger's dark skin, like some kind of blaze. Or a mark of the devil.

The clerk shuddered. He couldn't help himself.

Gabe Conrad lifted the rifle to his shoulder and sighted out through the open door, pretending not to notice the clerk's reaction. He'd seen the same thing a thousand times in the ten years since a cavalry captain had tried to run him through with a pitchfork, and it always reminded him of things he wanted to forget.

"—whole new standard in firearms," the clerk was saying. "I'm certain of it. They took their damn good time designing this piece, but I'm betting Winchester will be *the* name in rifles. Look at this." He tapped his finger against the receiver. "Steel frame, my friend. Not brass. They built the Seventy-three so it'll take any kind of punishment and keep on shooting. Same for the shells." The clerk leaned forward, his eyes intent on Gabe's. "Which, by the way, are .44's, so you carry the same ammunition for the rifle and the new Colt revolver. And I'm talking *centerfire*, my friend. Not only more reliable, but more accurate to boot! What are you shooting now?"

"Sharps," said Gabe. It was the first word he'd said in the store.

"Well of course the Sharps is a fine weapon . . ." said the clerk.

Gabe was eyeing him closely.

"—a fine weapon *for its day,* you understand. But the Seventy-three reaches out just about as far and throws a ball that's practically as heavy. And it keeps throwing them as fast you can work the lever!" There was a light mist of perspiration on the clerk's forehead. "You hit what you're aiming at, my friend, and by God you hit it with all the killing power you need. You can knock down any son of a bitch you want at three hundred yards."

Gabe looked down at the clerk, at the way his scalp was shining through a thin layer of wispy blond hair. The man was no more than five and a half feet tall, with small hands and a small pointed chin, but there was a flush on his face and a bright look in his eyes as he took the rifle back from Gabe. He worked the lever and threw the carbine to his shoulder.

"Goddamn if that doesn't feel good!" he said, his small cheek pressed against the receiver. "You could swear it's alive, couldn't you? You could swear it knows what it's by-God made for."

Gabe held back a smile and wondered what the clerk's imagination saw above the sights. Maybe the little man was shooting at grizzlies or elk, or saving a beautiful woman from a gang of bad men.

The clerk saw Gabe watching him and handed the rifle back with an embarrassed laugh, his gaze sweeping down across the stranger's well-worn coat. It was obviously handmade, from what appeared to be a single piece of buffalo hide. It hung from Gabe's shoulders all the way to the floor.

"What exactly is your line?" said the clerk. "Contract hunting?"

Gabe shook his head.

"Looking for work, then?"

Gabe shook his head a second time. "Just passing through."

"Can't say as I blame you, my friend. Nothing much happens in Nebraska. I bet you're going up to Deadwood to try your luck." The little clerk's eyes were even brighter than before. "I know that's where *I'd* go."

"Even if you didn't belong there?"

"Who says so? People are making fortunes every day. If I didn't have this business to run and a wife to tie me down . . ." The clerk's voice trailed off for a moment and then he said, "What? Why are you looking at me like that?"

"Ever hear of the treaty they signed at Fort Laramie?"

"Oh, that," said the clerk. "Sure. But who cares about a treaty with a bunch of savages when they're finding gold in the goddamn grassroots?"

"If they are then it belongs to the Lakota."

"The *gold?* You mean to say you'd turn over all that gold to a bunch of goddamn . . ."

The clerk ran out of words again. The stranger's eyes were still blank and empty, and yet they made the clerk nervous. He chewed the inside of his lip and studied the buffalo hide coat. He was thinking that the man's face didn't look like an Indian face, and his hair was light enough—about the color of dry sand—but the clerk was also noticing that the stranger wore his hair long and straight down over his shoulders, like some kind of Sioux brave. Then there was his skin, which was not only dark but also kind of leathery. And those damned moccasins.

"Are you," the clerk said, "I mean—don't get me wrong, my friend, but are you by any chance . . ."

There was a pounding of boot heels along the boardwalk out front and then another man came through the door, blocking most of the light. Gabe had an immediate impression of size, first, and then of anger; the man bearing down on them was even taller than Gabe's six-foot-two, and his green eyes flashed with a wild gleam of rage.

Gabe's hand moved by reflex toward the front of his coat but he could see that the big man's only interest was the clerk. Gabe looked puzzled but his next instinct was to back away, leaving the two men to take care of whatever it was that lay between them.

The clerk stepped back, too, but the big man had already reached the display case. He reached out across it with an arm like a tree branch and grasped a handful of the clerk's suit coat. The man's small body flew into the air at the end of the arm, arcing up and over the display case and then sailing into a corner of the store. The newcomer followed close behind, towering over the crumpled figure on the floor.

"You slimy bastard," he said. "You couldn't even face me, could you?"

"Mr. Haywood!" the clerk cried. "Please, I beg you—"

The man named Haywood pulled back his foot as if he wanted to smash the little man's ribs. Then he snorted and reached down and yanked the clerk to his feet. Gabe watched with a grim look on his face. He hadn't felt any great friendship toward the clerk, and anything he had felt was disappearing with the man's display of craven terror. But Haywood was proving himself to be an even greater coward by attacking an enemy who was so clearly helpless. All of Gabe's boyhood training told him to stay out of this fight between two grown men, that intervening would only bring them shame and humiliation. But he stepped forward when Haywood cocked one huge fist, holding the clerk's collar in the other.

"Don't do it," Gabe said.

Haywood glanced around with a flash of green eyes but he

wasn't really seeing anything. He drew his fist back a little further, about to strike.

Gabe was ready for that. He had gauged the mindless fury of the big man's anger, guessing that Haywood would not listen to reason. So the Winchester was already spinning and blurring in his hands. He slashed the barrel down across the knuckles of Haywood's upraised fist before the big man could launch his blow. Haywood grunted and let go of the clerk, clasping his injured hand while he whirled and lunged at Gabe.

But Gabe had expected that as well. He ducked low and took a new grip on the rifle, swinging the barrel down for a hard smashing blow against the side of Haywood's knee. This time the big man cried out, clutching his leg as he collapsed and rolled on the floor. In the next instant he was grabbing for the revolver on his hip, but he winced with pain when he tried to work the fingers of his gun hand.

Just as Gabe had known he would. That had been his reason for using the rifle barrel on Haywood's hand, instead of choosing a larger and easier target. Gabe had wanted to avoid gunplay if he could. It was an old habit to make such a series of strategic judgements and decisions—all of which he could have explained if anyone had asked—and to make them in that instant of deciding to act.

Haywood gave up on his right hand and rolled over to free his left, but Gabe had enough time to work the Winchester's lever action. It made an authoritative clacking sound and then the big man found himself staring into a rifle bore nearly half an inch across, holding rock steady just three inches above his right eye. Haywood had his left hand on the butt of his pistol by that time, but he was lying on his back and in pain and he was finally ready to think a little more clearly. He froze in place, the focus of his eyes traveling up the rifle barrel until he and Gabe were staring at each other.

"You're making a serious mistake," said Haywood.

"I'd be surprised," said Gabe. "It's been more than ten years since I've made a mistake."

Haywood narrowed his eyes, studying and weighing Gabe with a careful look. The blind rage was gone and Gabe could see now that the man would make a dangerous enemy. Haywood twisted his head slowly toward the clerk, who was still crouched in the corner. "What did you do, Tomlin, hire yourself a gunslick?"

"Oh no, Mr. Haywood, I wouldn't do that." The clerk was struggling to stand on shaky legs. "No sir, this man is just a customer."

"Then why the show?"

"I don't know," said the clerk. He glanced fearfully from Haywood to Gabe and back again. "He was just looking at the rifle, that's all."

Haywood slowly turned his head and once more Gabe felt the full force of his sharp green eyes. The fingers of the big man's left hand were still wrapped around the butt of his pistol.

"Then the Winchester ain't loaded," said Haywood. "You wouldn't keep a loaded rifle for customers to fool around with."

Gabe pressed the tip of the barrel against Haywood's cheek, brushing the big man's lower eyelashes with the front sight. "You might be right," said Gabe, as if he was curious about it himself. "Should we find out?"

Haywood studied Gabe's face, and for a while there was only the sound of a clock ticking somewhere in the store. "Well, shit," the big man said with a frown. "I'd hate to be sitting across from you in a high-stakes poker game."

There was no fear in Haywood's eyes and Gabe was sure now that he had underestimated the man. He saw how badly Haywood wanted to call his bluff and he began to wonder if he would have to drop the rifle to go for the gun under his arm. Haywood kept watching him, still gripping the pistol while the clock ticked away. Then his body relaxed and his hand eased away from the holster.

"Ain't no point," he said, talking more to himself than anyone. "Always another time."

"Always," said Gabe.

Haywood clambered to his feet and glanced at the clerk, who scuttled back toward the corner. When he looked at Gabe again there was something new in his eyes, something that looked like humor.

"Ten years and no mistakes is a damn fine record," he said.

"No serious ones, anyway."

There was a twitch at the corners of Haywood's lips. "Well, I hope you don't go and spoil things," he said. He waited a moment, watching Gabe, but he didn't get an answer. He shrugged and turned his back to walk toward the door.

He never gave the clerk another glance, but the clerk stared at Haywood's back until it was out of sight.

Gabe let the hammer down on the Winchester and that was enough to bring the clerk out of his reverie. He studied Gabe with a thoughtful expression that turned itself into a look of awe.

"My God," he said, "you didn't even work up a sweat."

"I didn't *do* much."

"Oh, no? You just stood up to Frank Haywood, that's all. Maybe the toughest, hardest man in this part of the country, and you tamed him like a pet mouse."

"He lives around here?"

"Practically *all* around. Haywood's got acreage on every side of Sidney except the East."

"He's a rancher?"

The clerk nodded distractedly, sighing deeply and pulling out a bright blue handkerchief to mop his forehead. "My God," he said. "I don't know what stroke of fate brought you here, my friend, but I'll never be able to thank you enough. Anything I have is yours."

Gabe knew he was expected to mumble a few words of gratitude, but they didn't come easy. He was feeling mostly contempt for the clerk, and the kind of embarrassment you have for someone who doesn't know enough to feel it himself.

"Anything," the little man said again. "That rifle you're holding? It's yours. And a case of shells, of course. And a Colt for your sidearm."

"That Haywood was pretty mad," Gabe said. It was the closest he could come to asking the question he wanted to ask.

"Nothing to worry about," said the clerk, waving the handkerchief in a gesture of dismissal. He went around behind the display case and bent down to reach inside. "Just a mixup over accounts. Now these are the shells for the Winchester, and here's the Colt I was telling you about."

"You don't expect more trouble?"

"From Frank Haywood? He's got a bad temper, maybe, but that's all. I appreciate your asking, my friend, but don't worry. I can clear it up." The clerk held out the revolver while he squinted at the opening in Gabe's coat. "I can't tell if you're carrying a sidearm or not, but it's always a good idea in this day and age."

"I've been getting along just fine with a Remington."

"You mean the old Army model?"

Gabe nodded. "Has a rugged frame. I like the strap over the cylinder."

"Same as the Colt," said the clerk. "Has it been converted?"

Gabe shook his head.

"You mean it's still percussion?"

Gabe nodded.

"Get rid of it!" the clerk said. "My God, didn't you hear what happened to McCall last month?"

"McCall?"

"The man who killed Hickok. He tried to shoot at the people coming after him but every other load was a god-damned dud."

"That just means he didn't take care of—"

"And even if you did have it converted you'd still have to carry .36 caliber shells. You'd always have to remember which shells went in which weapon. With the Colt you just stuff some ammo in your pocket and forget about it. And feel pretty damn safe, too." Gabe hesitated and the clerk held the Colt out a little further. "Please," he said. "You'd make me feel a lot better."

"These are yours to give?" said Gabe. "You're the owner here?"

The clerk stood a little straighter, looking pleased. "That's right, my friend. It's not much of a place, maybe, but it's all mine."

Gabe didn't feel like he had a choice. He'd been taught in childhood that refusing a gift insulted the giver. He knew that the whites saw things differently, but no matter how long he had lived among them it was hard to forget the old ways. He accepted the revolver with a nod of thanks.

The clerk kept his right hand out. "Name's Chester Tomlin, by the way. Pleased to make your acquaintance."

Gabe shook his hand but there was no pleasure for him in knowing a man like Chester Tomlin. There was only a dull ache that felt like loneliness and disappointment. He let go of the hand as soon as he could.

"Gabe Conrad," he said, turning to go.

CHAPTER TWO

Gabe hesitated just inside the hardware store, remaining in the shadows while he examined several open windows and the mouth of an alley across the street.

"I don't think you have to worry," said the clerk.

Gabe turned to look at him.

"I mean, worry about Mr. Haywood's intentions."

Gabe didn't say anything.

"Don't get me wrong," the clerk stammered. "I didn't mean to imply that you're afr . . . that he's a better . . . you know, that—"

"I understand," said Gabe.

The clerk closed his eyes in relief and Gabe went back to studying the street, ignoring his assurances. Once upon a time he had failed to ask himself why an unfriendly Army captain would get him released from the stockade at Fort Laramie. As a result he had not been prepared when the captain tried to kill him with a pitchfork in the post stable. The puckered scar and broken finger would always remain a bitter reminder of his carelessness, and now he never failed to consider all the possible meanings or results of anything that happened to him.

"I tell you he's not out there," the clerk insisted. "Don't you believe me?"

"What makes you so sure?" Gabe said without turning around. "He just about put you under."

"Not Mr. Haywood," the clerk scoffed. "He's a hard man but he's not an assassin. Folks respect him around here."

"Maybe you're right," said Gabe. "I don't see any sign of him."

Gabe went out to his pony and tied the Winchester to the side of his saddle. He would decide later how to pack it and what to do with the Sharps in his scabbard. The Colt and the shells went into his warbag. Finally he unhitched the pony and led it up the busy main street of Sidney.

He felt the clerk's eyes on his back the whole time.

Or the man who had *looked* like a clerk, but who apparently owned the store. The same man who claimed he wasn't worried about Frank Haywood.

Gabe started thinking about what he had seen in the shop, then frowned in irritation and shook his head as if to clear it. He would keep one eye peeled for the big rancher—he couldn't break the habit of being careful even if he wanted to—but otherwise he didn't see any point in trying to understand what had happened. Gabe didn't expect to see either man again because he had already decided to put the town behind him as soon as he could. He had come into Sidney only an hour before, looking for some company and a little fun, but that had been spoiled by the sour feeling that came over him when he shook Chester Tomlin's hand.

It was a familiar sensation, a disappointment that repeated itself over and over. Gabe hungered for something in other men, a sense of honor or pride or power that would make him feel he was not alone. As he wandered from place to place he looked for a spirit that would match his own. What he usually found were weak, greedy and small-minded men.

They were all around him now as he led his pony up the street. Sidney was one of the main jumping-off points for prospectors going to the new gold fields in the Black Hills, so it was a wild bunch of men who jammed the stores and lingered on the sidewalks. Gabe had enjoyed the noise and activity when he'd first arrived, but now he saw only the raw tempers and lust for gold. He wanted nothing more than to get away from the gamblers and prospectors and whores and all the other get-rich-quick artists.

Gabe had come into town covered with trail dust, looking forward to a hot bath and cool linen sheets. Now he longed for the solitude and silence of the prairie, a purifying sweat bath and a plunge in a cold stream. Later he could sit on the crest of a hill and meditate for a while, seeking guidance from *Wakan Tanka*. Perhaps the Great Spirit would show him in a vision how to overcome his unhappiness.

But then another kind of vision caught Gabe's eye, offering an answer to a more immediate problem. It was a sign in a saloon window advertising cold birch beer. Gabe's throat was as dry as the dust on his clothes, and even the drawing on the sign looked cold. Gabe hitched his pony to a rail outside.

A couple of drunks stumbled past him as he went through the door, as if the saloon had started to overflow with customers. It was a small place, probably built before the gold rush, and it was jammed with men who rubbed elbows and raw nerves almost every time they turned around. Gabe pushed through the crowd, smelling sour malt and sweat as he made his way toward the long bar on the right side of the room. There was no break in the line of men leaning against it, but some of them glanced up and then made room when they saw Gabe coming.

It was not an act of friendship. The men quickly looked away again and seemed to make a point of avoiding his eyes. Gabe knew that there was something about him that made most other men give him plenty of room. No one made a remark when he ordered his birch beer, nor while he tipped it back to savor the tangy bite of its fermentation.

Until he heard the sound of a woman's voice.

"You're making that look pretty good," she said. "Makes *me* wonder what I've been missing."

Gabe lowered his glass and turned around. A tall redhead stood behind him, eyeing him with an amused and faintly challenging smile. Gabe thought he had never seen a softer or more beautiful mouth. He realized she was standing nearly eye to eye with him and he was so surprised that his gaze drifted down over her body, as if he expected to see a pair of stilts strapped to her legs.

"Like what you're looking at?" the woman said.

Gabe met her eyes again. They were dark brown and filled with laughter. He nodded once in answer to her question before he let his gaze sweep over her again. The woman wore a scarlet satin dress, cut low and stretched tight across her full, rounded breasts. The fabric was cinched in tight around her waist to show that she was just as lean as she was tall, and also to emphasize the bountiful swell of her hips.

"Well I don't mind you looking," said the woman. "But sooner or later you have to say something."

Gabe realized he was staring at the woman's eyes again, entranced by the playful look he saw there. It was free of fear and full of life. "Why?" he said.

"What do you mean, 'why?' It's the custom."

"Why?"

"Because that's how people get to know each other."

"You mean it's the only way?"

"Well, we can't just stand around staring at each other all night."

"Why not?"

"Because we'd look pretty damn silly."

"Do you really care?"

The woman opened her mouth and then didn't say anything for a moment. Instead she gave him a thoughtful look that held even more interest than before. "Maybe not too much," she admitted, moving closer to him. "But now I'm getting a little curious about you. You're not like the other men who come through here."

"Thanks a lot."

"Did I say something wrong?"

He shook his head but the sour feeling was back. The mention of other men had reminded him of Chester Tomlin and the sullen bunch of drinkers who shied away from him at the bar.

"Then stop looking so glum." The woman pointed a long finger at his glass. "Maybe you could buy me one of those?"

Gabe pictured himself beside a crackling fire out on the prairie.

"Come on, be a sport," the woman teased, stepping in a little closer.

Gabe caught a whiff of her perfume and it made his head spin a little. It also made him think of wood smoke and the smell of fresh grass. "The thing is, I wasn't planning to—"

"Aw, don't go." The woman leaned even closer, her dress gaping open. "It's damn hard to find a man who's taller than I am and I like to make sure I have a chance to enjoy him when I do."

Gabe heard the promise in her words, and saw the swell of smooth white skin underneath the red cloth. It promised a lot more than he could see and he began to think about the way her breasts would fill his hands. "I guess I can buy a drink," he said slowly. "But I really wasn't planning to stay for long."

"Then let's start with the drink," the woman said with a grin. "We'll see what comes after that." She circled his arm with hers, squeezing it against her breasts. Gabe couldn't feel anything through the thick buffalo coat. He was thinking about taking the coat off when a hand snaked itself over the woman's bare shoulder and spun her away.

That's when Gabe caught sight of the man behind her, his long and narrow face sagging loosely with too much liquor. His eyes weren't dulled, however. They gleamed with a mean-looking fury. The man was already swinging his other hand as he tugged at the woman's shoulder, slapping her face before Gabe could react. The blow knocked her head to one side but she pulled out of the man's grasp and raised her chin to confront him with a defiant glare.

"Goddamn you for a two-timing bitch," said the man. He reached for her arm again and looked surprised when Gabe's fingers closed over his wrist. He tried to twist free, shifting his focus to Gabe. "You can stay the fuck out of this, you half-breed bastard. This is between me and Sarah."

The other drinkers edged away as soon as they heard the insult, but Gabe didn't react except for a kind of deadness that came into his eyes. It felt like the cold stillness that was also settling through his body.

"What the hell are you talking about?" the woman was saying. "There's nothing between us to start with."

"How can you say that, Sarah? After all the time you an' me spent out back?"

"I hate to tell you this, Harvey, but you weren't the only one."

There was a ripple of laughter at the bar and the long-faced man jerked his head around, straining against Gabe's grip while he glared fiercely at the men who were laughing. Then he focused on the woman again. "But I thought it was different with me."

The woman rolled her eyes but the laughter at the bar lost some of its humor. As if some of the men knew what it was like to feel that way.

"I guess I should'a knowed," Harvey said bitterly. "You ain't nothin' but a lowlife tramp."

"I thought you knew that when you *paid* me, Harvey."

There was more laughter but the man didn't seem to hear it. "That's all you are, then? Nothin' but a damned whore?"

The woman nodded, her face stiff. "That's what I am, Harvey. And you're a man who has to sleep with whores."

"Goddamned bitch!"

He tried to hit her with his other hand but Gabe yanked his wrist to pull him off-balance. Harvey continued his swing and shifted its aim to Gabe's jaw. Gabe easily blocked the flailing arm. He also let go of the man's wrist and slapped his face with an open palm. Harvey staggered back, massaging his jaw while he stared at Gabe with black-eyed hatred.

"How do you like it?" Gabe asked.

The man named Harvey swayed a little, giving thoughtful attention to the long buffalo hide coat. If Gabe was carrying any weapons they weren't right at hand.

"Tell me something," Gabe persisted, his voice as soft and empty as his eyes. "Is it just that you like hitting women? Or don't you have the courage to fight a man?"

"I don't fight the likes of you," said Harvey, his hand dropping suddenly to his side.

"No!" cried the woman. "Harvey—"

"I'll just shoot you down like—"

He didn't have a chance to finish. Gabe's right hand slipped up inside the coat, his broken finger curling over the trigger while the old Remington was sliding out of its shoulder rig. Some of the men around them were trying to scramble out of the way but it was over before they could react. Gabe's revolver came out under his left hand already sweeping back across the barrel. The hammer rose and fell and the blast caught the long-faced man in mid-sentence, with his own pistol only half out of its holster. His head jerked with the sound and then he looked down at his chest, at the blood pumping out through the hole torn in his heart. He kept looking at the spurting blood as he crumpled slowly to his knees and toppled over onto his face.

A heavy pall of white smoke swirled slowly in the still air, filtering stray shafts of sunlight. Someone murmured ''Jesus Christ!'' while others shook their heads or simply stared at Gabe, trying to fix in their minds the speed of the thing they had just seen.

Then a man stepped out of the smoke to come and stand over Harvey's body. He shook his head, too, his chest rising and falling with what appeared to be a heavy sigh. Gabe couldn't hear anything above the ringing in his ears, but he saw the sigh and then the dull gleam of light shining from a star pinned to the man's shirt. The star surprised him because the man's face looked mild, almost gentle, as if he was only someone's grandfather. Even his eyes, when the marshal lifted his head to look at Gabe, looked old and tired.

And yet, thought Gabe, this quiet man managed to show up at just the right time. It was something to remember.

The woman spoke first. ''It was self-defense, Sam. Harvey was—''

''I seen it, I seen it,'' the marshal said with a scowl, still eyeing Gabe. ''Tell me, mister, just exactly how long have you been in Sidney?''

''An hour?'' Gabe said with a shrug. ''Maybe an hour and a half.''

The marshal shook his head again. ''Hour and a half,'' he

repeated. "So all it takes you is an hour and a half to beat up on one of our leading citizens, then come in here and kill my best deputy."

Gabe felt Sarah looking at him but he kept his eyes on the marshal, still holding the Remington at his side. "So that explains why you're here," he said. "Frank Haywood went to you with a complaint?"

"Haywood!" said the woman.

"Well, of course he did," said the marshal. "What the hell do you expect? We been friends for nigh on fifteen years. So when he goes to see a man who's been cheatin' him—"

"Tomlin said it was just a misunderstanding."

"Tomlin," murmured the woman, rolling her eyes in disgust.

"Mister," said the marshal, "the only misunderstanding belongs to Chester Tomlin. He misunderstands how much he can get away with in this town. Even if he did hire himself a gunslick."

"I just happened to be in the store, if that's what you're talking about. I was looking at a new carbine."

"The one that's tied to your saddle out there?"

Gabe didn't say anything.

"You bought it, then?"

"It was a gift. For stopping Haywood."

"Aw hell," said the marshal, "Frank wouldn't of done much damage. No more'n Tomlin deserves, anyway."

"That's what Tomlin said. The first part, anyway. So there was no reason to hire any gunslick."

"I didn't really figure Tomlin hired you," the marshal said with a sigh. "That was Frank's idea and he was pretty worked up."

Gabe waited with a cautious look in his eye.

"But when he described you," the marshal went on, "I

figured I better come an' have a look myself. See if you really did have a broken trigger finger.''

Gabe expected the marshal to look down but the old man continued to hold his gaze and Gabe realized he had already seen it. He was clearly not as tired and worn out as he appeared.

"I believe you go by the name of Gabe Conrad," the marshal said.

"That's right."

There was a low murmur among the men at the bar, but the tone held more curiosity than knowledge or surprise. It made Gabe realize that most of the men were new to the West.

"—at least among the whites," the marshal said. "I think the Oglalas call you Long Rider."

Gabe didn't say anything. Neither man looked away.

"December twenty-first," the marshal said slowly. "Eighteen and sixty-six. That mean anything to you?"

Gabe nodded, partly in admiration and respect, but his eyes glittered with a bitter amusement. "Isn't that the day the Cheyenne and Lakota wiped out Fetterman and all his soldiers?"

The marshal's mouth looked tight. "That too," he said. "But I'm thinking about Omaha. The Stockman's Cafe."

"I think I remember something in the newspapers."

"Where'd you get that coat?"

"I made it."

"He was wearing a coat like that, the man who started the massacre."

"Massacre!" said Sarah.

"Wasn't there a witness?" said Gabe. "A woman who said it was self-defense?"

"Ten people were killed!" said the marshal. "Including

an Omaha deputy and a retired Army captain burned to death in his own barn.''

The murmuring at the bar got louder as Gabe and the old marshal kept staring at each other, like two buffalo bulls trying to size each other up. If the marshal knew this much about the fight, then he also knew that no one had ever been able to take Gabe back to Omaha.

"I'm sorry about your deputy," Gabe finally said. "He didn't give me much choice."

"I know that," the marshal said. "He was the best man I had when he was sober but just about worthless when he was drunk. But damnit, you goaded him!"

"Maybe," Gabe admitted. "A little. But he was acting like a—"

"The point is, you smell of trouble." The marshal tilted his head toward the other men in the room. "An' I already got enough trouble with all these buckos who think they're gonna strike it rich."

There was a hearty chorus of agreement and a few cheers in the saloon, and the marshal scowled at the stupidity of men who didn't know when someone was making fun of them.

"Look," said the old man, "I just think it'd be a good idea if you kept movin', don't you?"

"Don't worry," Sarah broke in. "He told me he wasn't planning to—"

Gabe held up his hand to stop her. "I was buying the lady a drink," he said. "I don't really know what'll happen after that."

The marshal looked at Sarah, who glanced nervously at Gabe, then simply shrugged. "Well I can't hardly blame you," the old man grumbled. "But I hope you make it short and get on your way."

"I don't think you understand," said Gabe. "Unless you're planning to arrest me for something—"

"Don't force my hand," the marshal warned.

"—I mean anything that'll stick in front of a judge."

The marshal sighed and scratched behind one ear, glancing at the floor and his dead deputy. "Well, shit," he said, "if you put it that way . . ."

"Because if you're not planning to arrest me, then don't try telling me where to go or what to do."

The marshal's head came up. "I try to play fair and square," he said. "I'll let things go for now. But I'm tellin' you, don't fuck up while you're in my town."

Gabe stared back, his face impassive.

"You hear me?" said the marshal, the tired look completely gone from his eyes. "Don't fuck up. Because you won't like what happens if you do. Are you listening? Because Omaha don't mean shit to me."

CHAPTER THREE

Sarah pulled Gabe away from the bar as soon as the marshal was gone, leading him through the back door to a small shack behind the saloon. She didn't say anything until they were inside and Gabe had pulled off his coat. Then she put her arms around his neck and shivered, pressing herself hard against his chest.

"I'm sure glad that's over," she said.

"Which part? Getting slapped or seeing me kill Harvey?"

The woman pulled back to study his face, peering closely at him in the dim light that came through a single window under the eaves. "The whole thing, of course. It was horrible."

"You mean it didn't work out the way you wanted?"

"What the hell does that mean?"

"It just seems kind of convenient, I guess. Your making a play for me with ol' Harvey right there to watch."

The woman frowned for an instant. Then a glimmer of

understanding made her eyes look like dark chips of ice. "You son of a bitch!" she said. "You think I *planned* that? You think I needed *your* help to take care of a man?"

Gabe shrugged. "He did seem kind of orn'ry."

"Oh sure," said Sarah. "So it's only natural for me to get some two-bit trail hand to shoot him down for me. For all I know you could've been killed, but that doesn't matter to me because it's all just for fun, right? That's how I get along in this town. That's how I build up a reputation so men will come looking for me—by trying to get some of them killed. That's just good business, right? I only wish—"

"All right," said Gabe.

"—I only wish I could get the other girls to follow my example. Then we'd all—"

"All *right*, I said. I just had to know."

The woman clamped her mouth shut, her full lips pressed into a narrow line while her nostrils flared with the effort of her breathing. A burst of music came out of the saloon as the back door opened for a moment. Gabe listened to two sets of footsteps until he heard the soft laughter of a woman leading another man to one of the neighboring cribs.

Gabe looked around, his eyes better adjusted to the gloom. The shack was just long enough for a bed and a chest of drawers, and no wider than it was long. The one narrow window was placed high enough to provide a little ventilation and still keep things private. It seemed obvious that the little cluster of shacks had only been built for the saloon girls, and only since the Black Hills gold rush at that. Gabe could smell the sap that was still oozing from the fresh pine lumber. Burlap had been nailed to the walls and ceiling to catch the sap.

"Are you satisfied?" said Sarah.

"It's not exactly luxury, but it'll do."

"You know what I mean, damn it. Do you still think I planned all that?"

Gabe almost smiled. "I guess I never did, really. Seems like you can take care of yourself."

"You just remember that."

"Don't worry, I'm not planning on becoming one of your problems." Gabe laughed. "Besides, I'm just a two-bit trail hand, remember?"

Gabe kept grinning at the woman and the frost slowly melted out of her eyes. "Like hell," she finally said. "I know men better than that. You're no more a two-bit trail hand than I'm a two-bit whore." Sarah reached up behind her back and after a moment the top half of her dress fell away. She lifted her chin a little higher as she watched Gabe's reaction. "Are you satisfied with *these?*"

"Satisfied isn't the word," said Gabe. He slipped a hand beneath each of her breasts and lifted them to feel their weight. Sarah groaned when he squeezed them, and when he brushed the palms of his hands over her nipples she let her head fall back with a long sigh. Gabe kissed the soft white skin of her throat and felt it vibrate when she spoke.

"I sure hope you were planning to fuck me," she said.

Gabe nodded against her neck.

"You know what I want?" the woman said suddenly.

Gabe shook his head and Sarah lowered her chin, looking up at him through the tangle of red hair that fell across her forehead.

"I want to do it standing up," she said, squeezing his arms. "You're up to that, aren't you?"

"I'd say we've got too many clothes on at the moment."

Sarah laughed and began attacking the buttons on Gabe's shirt while he slid her dress down over the smooth skin of her hips. He felt them wiggle under his hands and then the dress fell in a small scarlet heap around the woman's ankles. Gabe's shoulder rig lay next to it a moment later, quickly covered by his shirt and trousers. He moved against her then, her breasts bobbing against his chest as he grasped her bottom and lifted her effortlessly into the air. The woman held on with one arm around his neck while she reached down to take his cock in her other hand.

"Oh, good," she said with a throaty laugh. "You're big *all over*."

Gabe eased her down and she spread her legs around him, guiding his shaft with her hand. She was ready for it, slipping over him in an instant, moaning softly and throwing her head back again while she wrapped both arms around his neck. She pulled his head down and held it against her breasts, moving herself up and down on the pivot of his hips. She arched her back and Gabe took one full breast in his mouth, as much of it as he could, circling the nipple with his tongue. Sarah's moans grew louder, the rocking more violent, and then she was crying out, squeezing him between her legs with one last long shudder. She sagged slowly in Gabe's arms, letting her head sink forward against his neck.

"You're not tired?" she whispered after a while.

"Not hardly."

"You make me feel almost dainty, Gabe. Not like some overgrown giant of a—"

"Don't talk like that," said Gabe. "You should be proud. You make all the other girls look sickly."

"Some of the men, too."

Gabe laughed and so did Sarah, for a moment. Then she looked sad.

"But that's the problem," she said. "A girl wants to *feel* like a girl."

"Maybe. But I'm sure glad you've got the things a woman

oughta have.'' Gabe held her up with one arm while he tried
in vain to cover a breast with his right hand. Sarah looked
down at the broken trigger finger and touched the lower joint
where it hooked over at a forty-five-degree angle.

"What did the marshal mean about your finger?" she
asked. "Is that how he knew who you were?"

"It's a long story."

Sarah looked down again and this time she saw the scar.
She touched it gently, then took his hand in hers and turned
it over. "It goes all the way through," she said.

Gabe nodded and felt the woman shudder.

"It must have hurt terribly."

"I was too busy to notice at the time."

Sarah held his injured hand to her lips and studied him for
a moment. Then she pressed the hand against her breast
again and started moving her hips against Gabe's. "You still
feel pretty hard," she said with a little smile. "Were you
waiting for anything in particular?"

"Just for you," said Gabe. "I had you figured for a
healthy appetite."

Sarah laughed and nipped at his neck. "You're too good
to be true, stranger. Remind me to worry about it when I can
think better."

"I'll try."

"But right now why don't you plunk me down on that bed
and do whatever you want."

"I'll try," Gabe said again, and felt the woman giggling
against his throat while he lowered her onto the bed. She held
onto his shoulders and massaged them with greedy hands,
pulling his chest down against her breasts. This time he let
himself give in to the pleasure, plunging as deep as he could
while Sarah begged for more, pleading with him to fuck her
as hard as he could. He was almost sorry when he felt

himself flooding into her. She arched beneath him and settled back with a long sigh, still clutching his shoulders.

"Don't move," she said softly. "Please? It feels so good to have a man covering me up like this."

"I wasn't planning on going anywhere," Gabe said gently. "And when I do go I'll probably just start thinking about coming back for more."

The woman didn't say anything so Gabe raised himself up to look at her, frowning at the worried look on her face.

"You're not staying in Sidney," she said. "Are you?"

"You've given me a good reason to."

"I guess I should say thanks, but—do you really think it's a good idea?"

"I don't think the marshal will bother me, if that's what you're talking about. I think you called him Sam?"

The woman nodded. "Sam McClure. But it's not just him. Wasn't there some kind of a run-in with Frank Haywood?"

"Nothing serious. I hit him a couple of times."

"Nothing serious! No one's *ever* laid a hand on Frank Haywood before. So you make him look bad and call it nothing serious? He'll hate you for it."

"He won't be the first."

"But don't forget what Sam said. Those two have been friends forever. So now you've not only got a man who hates you, but you're in a town where his oldest friend is the law. Not to mention that you killed Sam's favorite deputy."

"Sounds tricky," Gabe admitted.

"Exactly!"

"And kind of interesting."

"This isn't a game, damn it! You could get yourself killed here."

"Only the rocks live forever."

Sarah was getting ready to say something but she stopped and gave him a curious look. "The Indians say that, don't they? Are you part Indian, like Harvey said?"

"That's not exactly the way he said it. But the answer is no, at least not exactly."

"Not exactly?"

Gabe eased himself out of her and rolled off to the side, his grey eyes losing their expression. "My parents were both white," he said. "But my mother lived with . . . well, she was captured by the Lakota before I was born."

"And your father?"

"He was killed when my mother was taken."

"I'm sorry, Gabe."

"Don't be. It was a good life for a boy."

Sarah heard the tone of rebuke and looked down at the hand resting on her belly. She covered it with her own and Gabe felt as if it was being bathed in heat.

"Did you get these wounds in battle, Gabe?"

"Sort of. Except that I was living with the whites by then and it was a white man who tried to kill me. Some friends of his took me to a livery stable and boxed me in while he tried to run me through with a pitchfork."

"My God," Sarah gasped, squeezing his hand tighter against her breasts. "Did he have a reason?"

"He thought so." Gabe laughed, making no effort to hide the bitterness in his tone. Then he shrugged. "It was one of those things that gets out of hand, I guess. I was just a kid, a stable boy at Fort Laramie. I'd been taken away from the Lakota and I didn't have much use for whites, especially the soldiers. Especially this one soldier who liked to abuse his horses."

"Some of them abuse their women, too."

"So you understand," said Gabe. "Well this particular soldier told me to get his pony one night when I was pitching hay. I was sixteen. But I could see he was drunk and I tried to talk him out of riding because I felt sorry for the pony. He could probably tell what I was thinking. Anyway, he tried to hit me and I didn't want him to.'' Gabe looked grim. "Who knows, maybe he really thought I meant to kill him. He was lying on the ground and taking out his gun when I tried to stop him the only way I could think of—pinning his arm down with the pitchfork. One of the prongs went through his wrist.''

Sarah groaned. "Probably served the bastard right,'' she said. "So he took the pitchfork away and tried to kill you?''

Gabe shook his head. "That was later, after I'd spent three years in the stockade. The captain changed his story and they let me out. I had a feeling something was up but I didn't think it through the way I should have. So those friends of his caught me alone and dragged me into the barn.'' There was a sad and distant look in Gabe's eyes. "I'd give anything if I could only go back and do it over. I'd call him 'sir' and give him whatever he wanted.''

"Why?'' said the woman. "You're here. You survived.''

"Sure, but—''

"Come to think of it, how did you get out of that stable?''

"Partly by doing what no one expected. I held out my hand to stop one of the thrusts and took a prong through my palm.''

Sarah shuddered, still squeezing his hand against her breasts. "That explains the scar,'' she said. "But what about the captain's friends?''

"I used the handle to knock them down.''

"With your hand still impaled on the prong?''

"There wasn't any time to take it out. Not with five men trying to pull weapons out of their holsters. I probably wouldn't be here now if it weren't for Bridger—''

"*Jim* Bridger?''

Gabe nodded. "He's the one who put me there, in a way, since he's the one who took me away from the Oglalas. But it turned out that my mother wanted him to. He also tricked Captain Price into getting me released, then helped me get away."

The woman was looking confused. "You make it sound as if your mother was still living with the Indians."

Gabe nodded. "She'd seen the way things were going and she wanted me to live among the whites. But she didn't believe she could return herself."

"It might have been hard," Sarah agreed. "There are certain attitudes people have . . ."

"I know."

"Did you go back to her, then?"

"To her and to my people. I purified myself and sought a vision. Then I married the woman I had desired as a boy."

"What was her name?"

"Yellow Buckskin Girl."

"You must have been happy."

"For a few days, on the journey to the Arapaho village where my mother was visiting relatives. The night we arrived was the happiest time I've ever known."

Sarah frowned at the joy and sorrow that mingled in Gabe's expression. "What happened?" she said.

Gabe sighed. "The soldiers attacked the next morning. Captain Price was there. He shot my woman in the head and ran my mother through with his saber."

"Oh, no!"

"He knew I was watching."

The woman made a sound of anguish and buried her face against his neck, circling his arm with hers. "Now I understand why you wish you could do it over."

"But I can't," Gabe said in a flat tone. "No one can. We can only go forward."

He felt a sudden tightness in the grip on his arm. Then the woman lifted herself up on one elbow and stared at him with wide brown eyes. "The Stockman's Cafe," she said. "Sam mentioned an army captain, didn't he? One of the men killed in the massacre?"

Gabe nodded, watching her closely. "It was the same man, as a matter of fact. Captain Stanley Price. He was killed in Omaha just like the marshal said."

Sarah moved away, pushing her back against the wall. "But ten people . . ."

Gabe's grey eyes glinted like polished granite. "I heard that Price killed three of them himself, and someone working for him killed the deputy. I think the rest were working for him too."

" 'You heard,' " Sarah echoed. " 'You think.' "

Gabe shrugged. "People have been telling stories about that day for a long time. They say Price was out of the army by then. He had a lot of men working for him, but no one knew exactly what they did. Three of them were in the Stockman's Cafe one night when the captain was eating dinner. All sitting at different tables for some reason." He looked at the woman to make sure she recognized the makings of a trap. "Then a stranger walked in and the three men drew their guns on him. The stranger killed them, but—"

"*All* of them?" said Sarah. "They drew first and you—well, the stranger killed them all?"

Gabe nodded. "Except for Price. He hid behind a woman and escaped out the back door. That's how the woman told it. She also said Price killed her husband when he tried to stop what was happening. Shot him down in cold blood."

"Jesus!" Sarah whispered.

Gabe didn't seem to hear her. He was grinding his teeth together and his voice was coming out in a thin harsh rasp.

"Price ran away," he went on, "and some more of his men were killed. Then Price got caught in that fire in the barn. Two more of his men were found outside. They were shot in the back, like they'd been trying to get away from him."

"He killed his own men?"

Gabe nodded solemnly. "No one ever saw the stranger again."

Sarah let out a breath she'd been holding for a long time, then touched Gabe's arm as if she was afraid to. "Did they ever . . . make any arrests?"

Gabe shook his head and Sarah continued to gaze down at him, searching his face.

"I said I knew men," she finally told him. "But this time I think I'm a little slow in catching on. I shouldn't be worrying about you at all, should I? If anything I should worry about Sam McClure and Frank Haywood."

Gabe shrugged once more. "Not if they don't cause *me* any trouble."

"I hope so," said Sarah. "They're good men. But does that mean what I think it means? Are you staying?"

"Maybe. You're the only one who can decide that."

"Me? How?"

"Well, if I stayed I would want you again—"

"I hope so!"

"—and *only* you."

The woman's eyes were puzzled for a moment, then thoughtful. "In other words, you want the same thing Harvey wanted."

"That's right."

"Sure," Sarah said immediately. "I'm yours as long as you want me. And no one else's." She looked down the length of Gabe's body. "Hell, I think you've spoiled me for other men anyway."

CHAPTER FOUR

Gabe picked a double Eagle off the stack of coins in front of him with just a trace of hesitation. The break in his movement was barely noticeable, like the shadow of doubt in his eyes. Then he tossed the twenty-dollar gold piece into the pot with a confident flourish.

"I'll just see your five," he said, "and raise it another fifteen."

The man to his left dropped out of the hand, as Gabe had hoped he would. He was a good-natured livery worker who couldn't afford to lose too much of his pay. But the sallow-faced man across the table was watching Gabe with a gleam of triumph in his eyes. Gabe felt a flush of satisfaction, although he met the man's gaze as if it was an effort—as if he wanted to look away.

"I guess I can stay," said the sallow-faced man, who went by the name of Mike Ravis. He tossed in a double Eagle of his own and followed it with two more. "But let's make things interesting."

Gabe's smile looked a little forced. Then he noticed
Chester Tomlin coming into the saloon and his mind drifted
for a moment. He hadn't seen the store owner for almost a
week, but he knew something was wrong from the way
Tomlin kept chewing his lip and twisting his hat in his hands.
Tomlin hovered near the table, catching Gabe's eye and
arousing his curiosity. Gabe had to force himself to concentrate on the game. He saw that the fourth player, a tall
redhead who had been sitting in since well before midnight,
was giving him a look of shrewd appraisal. The redhead
turned his cards over.

"I think I'll just watch this one," he said.

"Good," said Ravis. "That means it's between you'n me,
partner."

He was grinning in a way that was supposed to be friendly,
but Gabe could feel the malice behind it. The two men had
disliked each other from the start. Gabe thought Mike Ravis
was the kind of man who would throw his weight around and
run the other way if things got rough. He looked mean-
spirited and, even worse, he looked weak. Gabe instinctively
despised him for it.

"Well?" said Ravis. "What's your move?"

Gabe shrugged. "I might as well see your cards," he said.

The sallow-faced man watched him pushing more coins
and paper money into the pot. Then he sighed and shook his
head, giving Gabe a mock-regretful look. "I hate like hell to
do this," he said, "but now I think my hand's worth more
than that."

"Hey!" said Gabe.

"Now, now, my friend, I'm sure you know the rules of
poker. *I* know you want us to think you've got another
diamond in the hole, but you know you don't. Yes sir, I think
the situation calls for a second raise."

Gabe didn't say anything. Chester Tomlin stood behind

the man, twisting his hat harder than ever while the redhead sat back and studied Gabe with his head tilted to one side. Ravis pushed two more double Eagles into the pot.

"It'll cost another forty to see my cards," he said, the unfriendliness more apparent in his smile. "Unless you just want to get it over with and admit you're bluffing."

"That's what you think?" said Gabe.

"That's what I *know*."

Gabe nodded. "Then I guess you won't mind putting up another hundred to back your words," he said reasonably. "That's *my* second raise."

He pushed the money to the center of the table, and noticed that the redhead was grinning. Ravis looked at his own pile of coins and bills, then glared at Gabe. He knew he would look foolish if he backed out now. But it would be worse if he took a chance and stayed in, and threw away another hundred dollars. He studied Gabe's face for a long moment.

"No," he finally said, "you're still bluffing. You're good, I'll admit that much. You almost had me fooled. But there were too many little signs—"

"Does that mean you're in?" said Gabe.

"I'm in, damn you! Let's see it."

Gabe started to say something. Then he shrugged and flipped his hole card face up. Red diamonds showed bright against the green felt.

"You son of a bitch," said the sallow-faced man. "You tricked me!"

He jumped to his feet, his chair crashing to the floor behind him. A dozen conversations stopped at once and a few drinkers edged away from the line of fire. Everyone in the room heard Gabe's next words even though he was barely speaking above a whisper.

"Just how did I manage that?" he said.

"You made it look—made it look like . . ."

"In other words I bluffed you?" Gabe said mildly.

"Not the usual way. You made it look . . . well, you know what I'm talking about. I'll be damned if you take that pot."

Gabe stared at the man, restraining the urge to kill him outright. He had learned how to accommodate himself to the white man's idea of murder. "Not only am I going to take that pot," he said slowly, "but you're going to put in the last hundred dollars you agreed to."

"Like hell I am." The man's hands hovered near his waist. "You just try and get it."

Gabe shook his head. "You didn't hear me, I guess. *You're* going to put it in. Either that or use those guns."

Gabe hadn't moved a muscle since he'd turned over the card. He was still stretched out casually in a captain's chair, eyeing the man who stood across the table trying to make up his mind.

"But if you reach for them," said Gabe, "I'll kill you."

Mike Ravis kept staring at him, thinking that the dark stranger with the grey eyes couldn't possibly be that fast. He was also thinking about what would happen if he backed down. He'd be laughed out of town. Then he took a closer look at those pale eyes and thought, *Hell, there's always other towns.* He separated his holdings, pocketing what was left before he threw a handful of coins and folding currency on the table. His mouth twisted in a contemptuous sneer.

"I pay my debts," he said. "But I'll be seeing you again."

"I doubt it," said Gabe. "You don't have the balls."

The man's black eyes glittered with hatred and Gabe thought he'd pushed him too far. But Ravis only wheeled and stalked out of the saloon. The conversations picked up again, full of excitement and speculation. The redhead gathered the cards with a grin on his face and started shuffling. Chester Tomlin came toward Gabe, fumbling with the hat in his hands.

"Could I talk to you?" he said.

"Sure."

"Privately? Could I buy you a drink?"

Gabe looked at the store owner's bowed head, torn between a feeling of distaste and a sense of obligation. The silence made Tomlin look up from his hat. His eyes were red-rimmed and full of suffering.

"I guess I can quit while I'm ahead," Gabe told him. "Come on, let's find a table."

Chester Tomlin ordered a whiskey at the bar. Gabe stuck with birch beer. The store owner gave him a quizzical look, then followed him toward an empty table. Tomlin was shaking his head as they sat down.

"You sure take chances," he said.

"When?" said Gabe.

The store owner saw that he was genuinely puzzled. "At the poker table, of course. Mike Ravis has a bad temper and he knows how to use that gun."

"But who said I was taking chances?"

Tomlin laughed. "I'm sorry, I should know better after the way you handled Frank Haywood." He gulped half of the whiskey in his glass, then fixed his eyes on Gabe's. He looked a little more hopeful. "That's why I'm here, actually. I need help and you're the only—"

Gabe frowned.

"I know," Tomlin said quickly. "I don't have any right to ask. You've already saved me from a beating and here I am, asking for more. But I don't have any choice, Mr. Conrad. I'm in trouble and you seem like a man who can handle trouble."

"Isn't that what the law is for?" Gabe pronounced the

word *law* as if he didn't have much use for it. "I heard you don't get along too well with the marshal, but I thought—"

"He said he'd kill her."

"Kill who?"

"My wife."

"The *marshal?*"

"The man who has her! He'll kill her if I go to the law."

"You mean someone ran off with your wife?"

"They took her by force, Mr. Conrad. Right out of our home. I came back for supper and she was gone."

"Tonight?"

Tomlin nodded. "They must have taken her this afternoon."

"Then how do you know what happened? How do you know it was a man who—"

"He left a note. Telling me how to get her back."

"A coward!" said Gabe, his indifference turning to anger. "He threatens an innocent woman to get what he wants?"

Tomlin nodded again, watching Gabe's expression.

"Do you know who it was?"

The store owner looked away. "Not exactly," he said. "I mean, I don't know who it was that took my wife and left the note."

"What did it say?"

Tomlin looked at Gabe again. "It asks for money, mostly. I have to bring the money to a certain place, just before sunset tomorrow."

"So the coward can hide in the dark," Gabe snarled. "Will you do it?"

"I have no choice." There was anguish in Tomlin's voice and a pleading look in his eyes. "But what if it isn't enough?"

"Is that why you came to me?" said Gabe.

"What if the man doesn't let her go? What if he's afraid to? She'll know who he is."

"Where will you leave the money?" said Gabe.

The store owner slumped back in the chair and bowed his head, his scalp shining through a thin layer of blond hair. "I know there's no reason you should help me," he mumbled. "But I'd be glad to give you—"

"I asked about your instructions. Where are you supposed to go?"

The store owner's head snapped up. He blinked his eyes, then swallowed the rest of the whiskey in his glass and started talking fast. "Do you mean it?" he said. "Oh Lord, I was afraid to even hope. But if there's really something you could do, Mr. Conrad, you'd have my eternal gratitude. Believe me, anything I own—"

"That's not necessary," said Gabe.

"But I mean *anything*. Guns. Money. You name it and it's yours."

"I have all I need."

"Then why—"

"For the woman," said Gabe.

"But you don't even know her."

"And because I want the man who hides behind a woman's skirts."

The words came out with such force that Tomlin shrank back, blinking his eyes again. "I'll still be thankful," he said uncertainly. "But you're sure there isn't . . . that I can't—"

"Just tell me what will happen tomorrow."

The store owner scratched the side of his neck, studying Gabe with a quizzical frown. "Well, I'm supposed to go north on the Black Hills road. There's a grove of trees about eight miles out."

"Does the road pass through the trees?"

"No, they're down in a wash. I'll just sort of wander into them with a bag and come back without it."

"You think the man will be watching?"

"You know the country around here," Tomlin said with a shrug. "Lots of rolling grassland. You can see things a long ways." He noticed Gabe's frown and said, "Why? What are you thinking?"

"Is there anything near the trees?" Gabe said. "Anyone living nearby?"

"Not that I can think of. Why?"

Gabe was staring into the shadows that flickered in the rafters above the coal oil lamps. "Even so," he said, speaking more to himself than to Tomlin, "I don't think he'd get too far away from the woman."

The store owner gave him a dubious look. "You're not planning to search the area, are you? What if he saw you first and thought—"

"Can you give me food?" said Gabe. "A day's bread and meat. And water?"

"Sure, but what about—"

"Trust me, Mr. Tomlin. There will be two who watch you deliver the money, and one to watch the other pick it up."

The store owner nodded slowly, thinking it over. "Well sure," he said. "That might work. The moon's almost half full and you could see things pretty well. But what if he's already there? What if he sees you looking for a hiding place?"

"Will he be watching in the dark?"

Tomlin stared. "You mean you'd go tonight? But how would you keep your horse hidden all day tomorrow? It's nothing but grass out there and you can't even use the ridge, since you don't know what direction—"

"Who said anything about a horse?"

"How the hell would you get there? How would you follow him?"

Gabe shrugged. "You said the grove was only eight miles away."

"Only!"

"I'll be there before the sun comes up. As for following, that'll be much easier on foot anyway. Less noise, less dust, less chance of being seen. And I don't think the coward will be going far. I'm still sure he's keeping your wife close by."

"I hope so for your sake."

"I'm also sure he had a horse for your wife, to make it look more natural."

"But what about you?" said the store owner. "That still leaves you stuck out in the middle of nowhere."

Gabe looked at him. "Don't forget that this man will have a horse," he said. "After tomorrow night he won't need it anymore."

CHAPTER FIVE

The sun burned its way across a white-hot sky while Gabe lay flat on his belly in the grass. There was no shade on the rim of the wash that Tomlin had described the night before. Stalks of dry grass pricked at Gabe's skin and ants crawled through the sweat on his legs but still he remained quiet, watching the grove of trees down below. This was the endurance and patience he had learned as a boy among the Oglalas, the people who honored him with the name of Long Rider for a daring act he performed in the winter of his fourteenth year. He had ridden two ponies to their deaths, fighting his way through a blizzard to warn another band of Lakota that soldiers were approaching their camp.

He had plenty of time to remember such things during the long hours of waiting above the pine grove. He was confident that he could not be seen unless someone rode right over top of him. Even twenty paces off in either direction and the tall grass would block the view.

The Sidney road cut across the wash on the other side of the trees, and all morning Gabe had watched a steady flow of wagons beginning the long journey to the Black Hills gold fields. The traffic had dwindled and disappeared in the afternoon, but the same could not be said for Gabe's bitter feelings toward the invaders. He remembered the sacred beauty of the mountains he had visited as a boy, the gentle slope of green meadows and the whisper of wind in the trees on the hillsides. The Lakota believed the mountains to be the center of the earth, the same mountains that white miners were ripping apart with their picks and shovels. Gabe felt a fierce pleasure in knowing that Crazy Horse was still free in the north and still fighting the whites.

Part of the pleasure was knowing that he had helped to make it possible. Gabe remembered the day he saved Crazy Horse from an ambush by Crow warriors. He and The Strange Young Man of the Oglalas had become fast friends and allies, until the day Gabe said goodbye to him for the last time. It happened only a few miles from the place where Gabe was hiding, and Crazy Horse had tried to warn against having any contact with whites. But Long Rider had burned with the desire to find the man who murdered his wife and mother.

He had found his mother's father first, a lawyer in Boston who believed that his daughter had died many years before. The old man had been overjoyed to learn he had a grandson. But he was dead now, too, leaving Gabe an estate that was worth many thousands of dollars.

Gabe did not fully comprehend the amount. He only knew that he could write a draft on a Boston bank whenever he needed to, and there was little chance of the well running dry. He had meant it when he told Chester Tomlin there was nothing he wanted.

Unless it was something he couldn't buy with money. He knew he was possessed by a powerful desire he couldn't quite name, a hunger that sometimes drove him to do things he didn't completely understand. Like walking eight miles just to lie on his belly all day in the grass.

He thought he had a little understanding of the hunger because sometimes, when he thought about the things that had happened to him, it seemed as if he was feeling sorry for someone else. Gabe's heart would ache for the boy named Long Rider who had been torn from his home and from the love of Yellow Buckskin Girl, only to find her again and see her die at his mother's side. It wasn't surprising that he tried to protect other children and other women whenever he found them being threatened.

Gabe's mood was still sour when a distant movement caught his attention. He squinted against the late afternoon sun and saw a single rider coming down from the upper end of the wash. Gabe glanced at the road, seeing that there were no travelers who might observe the approach, then turned his attention back to the rider. A cold fury was growing in his heart. *This is the man,* he thought. *This is the one who took an innocent woman from her home.* Gabe looked beyond the rider, studying a higher ridgeline behind him. *If the woman is still alive,* Gabe thought, *then that is where she is.*

The rider drifted toward Gabe's side of the wash and angled up the slope to walk his pony along the rim. Gabe had to lift his head a little higher to watch, until the man was so close that Gabe could hear the creaking of saddle leather. And still he kept coming closer. *I almost hope the bastard finds me,* he thought. *It'll give me an excuse to kill him right now.* Gabe knew it would be a mistake, but at least he'd enjoy making it.

The rider stopped less than a hundred feet away, near an

outcropping of white rock that Gabe had noticed earlier.
Gabe wasn't watching by that time. He was lying as flat and
still as he could, knowing that any movement in the grass
could expose his presence. He heard the man drop from the
saddle and lead his horse away from the rim of the wash, out
of sight from the road and trees. Then he heard the man
walking back, his legs brushing through the dry grass. The
man stopped suddenly and levered a Winchester or maybe a
Henry, the rattle exploding in the silence.

Gabe stopped breathing, every muscle tensed for the
impact of a bullet. It took all his self-control not to flinch or
roll out of the way. But Gabe knew the man could not have
seen him and so he waited, trying to picture what was
happening. He guessed that the rider was surveying the road
and the wash, looking for any sign of a trap. Gabe smiled
with grim satisfaction. Then he heard the sound of scuttling
stones and crunching grass as the man settled into a hiding
place of his own. Gabe relaxed slightly but he never stopped
listening. It was the only way he could keep track of the man
with the rifle.

At least an hour went by, the air finally turning cooler as
the sky faded from white-blue to grey. A breeze came up and
dried the sweat from Gabe's skin. Then he heard a low,
harsh laugh that sounded full of greed and anticipation, and
he knew that Chester Tomlin had appeared on the road down
below.

Nothing else happened for a while, even after enough time
had passed for Tomlin to leave his bag of scrip and disappear
back up the road. Gabe guessed that the rider was waiting for
the cover of night. If he was, he didn't have enough patience.
There was still some grey in the sky when Gabe heard more
rustling in the grass. The man's steps went away and turned
into the soft thud of a pony's hooves coming back.

Gabe hugged the ground even tighter, one hand on the butt of his Remington, until he was sure that the rider was going over the rim and down the side of the wash. He heard the horse running and took his first deep breath in a long time, lifting his head to look down the slope.

The rider was just disappearing in the grove of trees. He came back out a minute later, little more than a dark shape against pale grass in the gathering darkness. Gabe saw a lighter patch of color on the saddle that had to be Tomlin's bag of money. The rider paused for one last look around, then spurred his horse back up the wash.

Gabe waited a few seconds longer, carefully stretching his muscles before he got to his feet and ran down the slope. He followed the retreating shadow up the wash, knowing the rider wouldn't keep up his pace for very long. Gabe hoped to follow the sound of the horse after darkness fell, or wait for moonlight if he had to follow its trail of bent grass. Gabe ran along the bottom of the wash in an easy stride, dropping to his knees now and then to listen and maybe catch a glimpse of the rider's silhouette against the sky.

There was no sound when he kneeled the fourth time, and the rider's shape loomed up much closer than before. Gabe froze in place, fearing that the man had heard him running through the grass. Then a match flared and a peal of laughter rang out, and Gabe scowled. The outlaw had simply stopped to gloat over the contents of Tomlin's bag.

Gabe had grown up believing that wealth was counted in ponies and plenty of dried meat for the winter, acquired through acts of bravery and endurance. But the man he was following found pleasure in a bag full of colored paper, won at the expense of a frightened woman.

Gabe followed him with an even greater determination.

The outlaw was walking his pony now and Gabe was glad,

because the darkness was nearly complete and the moon hadn't come up yet. The faint glow of starlight was enough to keep him from stumbling over larger rocks, but the heavy soles of his moccasins were his only protection against prickly pear cactus. He stepped as carefully and as silently as he could, staying just a few yards behind the rider. The ground gradually leveled off and then a low hill was blotting out the stars in front of them. The sound of the pony's hoofs veered to the left, and Gabe stayed behind them.

The moon was waiting around the side of the hill, hanging low and yellow across a hundred miles of rolling grassland. Gabe drifted farther back in case the rider turned around. He guessed they had covered about three miles, but it looked as if the trip was nearly over. He saw the dark shape of a cabin nestled against the base of the hill, with a soft glow of lamplight in its window.

The rider stopped out front and climbed down while Gabe crouched in the grass to watch. There was a second horse tied to the corner of the cabin and something on the ground that might have been a saddle. But instead of putting the saddle on the horse the man loosened his own cinch strap, as if he didn't expect to be leaving for a while.

Gabe frowned at that, beginning to worry about the fate of Tomlin's wife. If the man was planning to return her, then it would make sense to do it during the night. Gabe was up and moving as soon as the rider went into the cabin, although he paused to listen just outside the door. He couldn't know for sure how many people were inside and he didn't feel like running into any surprises.

"It's all here," said a man's voice.

Gabe jumped a little, hearing the voice so clear and close in the deep night silence. He wondered if it belonged to the rider or an accomplice. He cocked his head and waited, but all he heard was the same harsh, greedy laugh he had heard before.

"All here and all mine," the voice said when it was done laughing. "All for about two days' easy work." There was a dull thump, like a bag of money being dropped on a table. "But I see you ain't impressed," said the man. "It ain't nothin' compared to all your momma's money. You think you got everything you need, right?" He laughed again. "Well it's time you found out what you been missin'."

Gabe heard the crunch of a straw mattress, followed by frantic thrashing and muffled cries.

"Cut it out!" said the man, his voice harsh with effort. "Christ, I was startin' to feel sorry for you. Why'd you ever marry that little runt?"

Gabe listened to the sounds of struggle a moment longer, then lifted the latch and stepped through the door with his Remington in his hand.

A woman was lying on her back on a mat on the floor, stripped naked, her mouth stuffed with cloth and her arms tied to a hook in the wall behind her head. Muscles stood out hard along her body as she strained against the rider, who was pressing himself down between her legs. Gabe thumbed back the hammer of his revolver and the man looked up, his face twisting with surprise. "What the fuck!" he said. "Where'd you come from?"

Gabe's finger tightened on the trigger but he held his fire when he saw the terror in the woman's eyes. He didn't want the man collapsing on top of her, spraying blood all over her body. He put the revolver back on his hip.

"Get up," he said.

The man glanced at a gunbelt just out of reach across the floor.

"*Now!*" Gabe roared.

He took a step toward the mattress and the man jumped to his feet. The woman rolled toward the wall and curled her knees to her chest.

"All right, all right," said the outlaw, pulling up his trousers. "I'm movin'. Just take it easy, mister." His hands shook and he had trouble getting his trousers buttoned. He was an older man, somewhere around forty, with small dark eyes and a broad, flattened-out nose. His hair looked greasy and his jaw bristled with several days of stubble.

"Maybe you want a little?" he said, nodding toward the woman. "She ain't all that pretty but hell, pussy's pussy." He grinned, showing broken teeth, and raised his eyebrows by way of invitation. "Plenty for both of us, stranger. Ain't no one gonna stop it."

Gabe grabbed a handful of the man's shirt and shoved him toward the door. He hadn't seen any blankets in the cabin so he used his knife to slice the rope binding the woman's wrists, trying to look the other way to prevent embarrassment. The woman stayed on her side and hugged her knees, either shaking or sobbing, but Gabe had to take care of the outlaw before he did anything else.

The man had stopped beside a table that held a flickering coal oil lamp and a yellow carpetbag with blue woven flowers. He glanced at the bag, then flashed a pleading look over his shoulder.

"Now hold on," he said. "Hear me out before—"

Gabe kicked him, swinging the bony part of his ankle as hard as he could up between the man's legs. He would have used his toes if he'd been wearing boots. The outlaw bent in half, holding his crotch and groaning in pain, then stumbled out through the door like a man trying to escape misery.

Gabe thought the man had another idea in mind and followed him outside. The man weaved toward his horse as if he wanted something to lean on in his suffering. Gabe nodded with satisfaction when the man made a sudden dash to the off-side, reaching for an old Henry repeater on the saddle.

The man was trying to use the horse for cover but the shape of his head was visible across the pony's back and that was all Gabe needed. He pulled the Remington again, with plenty of time to line up his sights in the light of the moon. His slug caught the man just over the right ear and punched a fist-sized hole through the other side of his head. The outlaw fell on one side of the horse and his rifle on the other.

Gabe heard a sharp cry above the explosion and ran back into the cabin. Tomlin's wife was on her feet and struggling with a muddy brown dress while she stared at the open doorway, her eyes wide with fear. Gabe had to admit that her face was kind of plain, but he couldn't help remembering how soft and well-rounded her body had looked in the lamplight. It made his voice sound a little husky.

"Don't worry," he said. "You won't be bothered anymore."

The woman relaxed a little, except for the work-worn hands clutching the dress against her breasts. The back of the dress was still hanging open. "Here," said Gabe, moving toward her, "turn around and let me help you with—"

The woman stepped back and Gabe hesitated, seeing the wary look in her eyes. He waited a few seconds longer but it didn't show any signs of easing up.

"All right," he said with a shrug. "You don't have any reason to trust me. But your husband sent me to—"

"My husband!" said the woman.

"Sure," said Gabe. "That's how I know you're Jane Tomlin. You are, aren't you?"

The woman nodded, watching him closely.

"Well, Mr. Tomlin wanted to make sure you weren't harmed," said Gabe. "He was willing to pay the ransom all right, but he was afraid of what would happen afterward. Looks like he was right."

Jane Tomlin didn't answer. Gabe waited for questions or maybe a fit of emotion, but she only studied him as if she was trying to make sense out of what he'd said—and having a hard time of it. He shrugged again, figuring the woman still suffered from the shock of nearly being raped.

"I'll go outside," he suggested. "I can saddle the horse while you finish dressing. I assume you're ready to go home?"

"Sure," the woman said. "Of course."

But her voice came out flat, as if she wasn't feeling much of anything, and Gabe gave her one more look before he turned away. He picked up the carpetbag on his way out the door and tied it to one of the saddle strings on the outlaw's horse. Then he put the Henry back in its scabbard, tightened the cinch strap, and saddled the second horse. Finally he dragged the outlaw's body around the side of the cabin, where Jane Tomlin wouldn't have to see it.

Not that he was all that sure she would mind if she did.

It was an easy ride in the moonlight, the ponies picking their way back around the hill and down the wash. When they had passed the dark grove of trees and reached the Sidney road, Jane Tomlin cleared her throat and thanked Gabe for saving her from the outlaw. Then she asked him how long he had known her husband. Gabe told her about the fight with Frank Haywood the week before, after which the woman lapsed into another silence that lasted the rest of the journey.

They came into the deserted streets of Sidney just before

dawn, the sound of their horses echoing between the dark buildings. They passed a cemetery and came to a large house on the other side. All the windows were dark but Chester Tomlin must have been waiting for them. The little storekeeper scurried out into the street with a lantern in one hand, holding it up toward his wife.

"You're safe!" he said. "Praise heaven, I can't believe my eyes! Did he do you any harm?"

"Harm?" said the woman. "He only stripped me and bound me and very nearly assaulted me."

"But you're alive, my dear! I was afraid to hope as much." Tomlin turned to Gabe, his scalp shining up through his hair in the circle of lantern light. "I don't know how I can ever thank you, sir. Did you have any trouble? Where did you find her?"

Gabe glanced at the woman. "He was using a cabin near the wash. You better tell someone to go out and get the body."

"Then he's dead," said Tomlin. "I wish I could've been the one to pull the trigger."

Gabe shrugged. "Probably doesn't make any difference to him."

"Did you recognize the bastard? What did he look like?"

"Like an old neighborhood tough from back East, come out to make his fortune. I never saw him before." Gabe glanced at the woman again. "Maybe we could put the horses away and go inside?"

"Of course!" said Tomlin. "I'm not thinking clearly. But this cabin you're talking about, was it east of the road?"

Gabe nodded. "Three or four miles, I guess. At the base of a hill."

"That's the one!" said Tomlin. "It'll be enough to get him arrested."

Gabe sighed, feeling the effects of two nights' lost sleep. "I already told you," he said. "The man who did this is dead."

"Not him. I'm talking about Frank Haywood."

"What's that?" said Jane Tomlin, suddenly coming alive. "I only saw one man and you just heard that it wasn't Mr. Haywood."

"Of course not," her husband sneered. "Not when it's so easy to hire some drifter to take all the risks. But that cabin belongs to Haywood. It's one of the line shacks on his ranch."

"Seems like anyone could borrow a line shack," said Gabe. "Especially in the summer when no one's using it."

"Then what about those horses you're on? Did you notice the brand?"

It was the first thing that most westerners would notice. "Sure," said Gabe. "I suppose you're about to tell me the Circle K is Haywood's brand?"

"None other," said the storekeeper.

"But the same thing applies," said Gabe. "Anyone can steal a couple horses."

"Maybe. But there's more." Tomlin nodded toward Gabe's saddle. "The clincher is in that bag."

"The money?" said Gabe.

"That and something else," said Tomlin. "You mean you didn't open it?"

Gabe shook his head. "Not much point. And anyway, it's your property."

"Well take a look now," said Tomlin. "You'll see what I mean."

Gabe studied the storekeeper for a moment, then untied the carpetbag from the saddle string and spread it open. There were several bundles of greenbacks inside, and a folded sheaf of papers on top. Gabe took out the papers and tilted them toward the lantern that Chester Tomlin was holding as high as he could.

"Looks like a deed," said Gabe. "Something you signed over to Haywood."

"Only because he demanded it," said Tomlin. "Only because he threatened to kill my wife if I didn't."

"I don't believe it," said his wife, reaching for the paper in Gabe's hand. "Can I see that?"

Gabe passed it across. "Looks like what he says, ma'am. A deed for a quarter section."

"Not just any quarter section," said Tomlin. "There's a spring-fed lake in the middle of that property."

Gabe nodded but the woman was looking confused.

"Cattle need water," he told her. "My guess is that Haywood wanted the lake so he could expand his range."

"Exactly," said the storekeeper. "There's good grass all around it."

"But he wouldn't do it this way," said the woman. "Not Mr. Haywood."

"Why not?" said Tomlin. "What's so special about Mr. Haywood?"

"Well nothing," the woman stammered. "But he has a certain reputation, you know. I just can't imagine . . ."

"You told me the same thing," Gabe reminded the storekeeper.

"I'm as surprised as you are," said Tomlin. "But I have the deed, don't I? I also have the note they left me. Which means I have the son of a bitch right where I want him."

"Are you sure it's enough?" said Gabe. "He's on pretty good terms with the law around here."

"*Town* law, yes. He and Marshal McClure are thick as thieves, if that old coot even knows what a thief looks like these days."

"Chester!" said the woman.

"But county law is another matter," Tomlin said with a grin. "Sheriff Harry Thorne is a friend of mine and *he's* the one with jurisdiction over Mr. Frank Haywood."

"But Chester, what about—"

"Don't worry, dear, I'm going to see Harry right now. I'll make sure Haywood's arrested before he can do any more harm. That *is* what you're worried about, isn't it?"

Jane Tomlin glanced from her husband to Gabe and back again, a troubled look in her dark brown eyes. "Well, of course," she said quietly. "Thank you for taking care of things, Chester."

CHAPTER SIX

Gabe came awake with the sound of knuckles pounding on a door, pounding the blackness of sleep out of his head. Then he felt a woman's breasts against his arm and he opened his eyes, letting them linger on the blankets clinging to the curves of Sarah's body. Chester Tomlin had offered him a spare bedroom but Gabe had said no thanks and headed straight for her little shack just as dawn was breaking. A boy had been swamping out the saloon in front and Gabe had made a deal with him. Now the knocking stopped and the boy's voice came through the door, sounding uncertain.

"Are you awake, sir? He's comin' in right now."

"Thanks," Gabe called out. "I'm awake."

"Better hurry," said the boy. "Someone seen 'em on the road. They'll get here any time."

Gabe was already pushing his legs into a pair of trousers. "Good work, son. I'm on my way."

"I wish you weren't," Sarah murmured. Her face was still half-buried in a pillow, letting him see only one saucy brown eye looking up through a tangle of red hair. She shifted her hips languidly beneath the sheets while half of a wicked grin showed above the pillow. "Can't I talk you into staying, lover?"

Gabe slipped a hand under the covers and between her thighs and for a moment he was tempted. Her skin felt like warm silk. Then he sighed and reached for a white linen shirt hanging from a chair. "Maybe you can talk me into coming right back," he said. "But I have to see this through."

"I'm glad, I guess. You're not the only one who wants to know how this turns out."

"I take it you still don't think Haywood was behind it."

The woman shook her head against the pillow. "Holding a man's wife as a prisoner? Just to get a piece of land?"

"An *important* piece," Gabe reminded her.

"It's still too tricky for a man like Frank Haywood. You saw the way he wades into things."

"I remember," Gabe said with feeling. "But why the demand for a deed in the first place, then? With his name on it? No one else could use it."

Sarah frowned and shook her head a second time. "I don't know, Gabe. It doesn't make any sense."

"That's nothing new. Everything's been a little cockeyed ever since I rode in." Gabe finished buttoning his shirt and reached for his boots, looking thoughtful. "Maybe it was just the money after all," he said. "There was something I forgot to ask you about when I came in."

"We did get a little sidetracked."

"I remember that too," Gabe said with a grin. "But what about Mrs. Tomlin having a lot of money? The man who took her said something like that just before I went into the cabin—like it belonged to her and not her husband."

"Yeah," said Sarah, nodding her head. "They say she's the next thing to rich, actually. Her mother died last year and she's the only child. Her father was already dead before that. So Jane Tomlin owns a factory and a couple of stores in Chicago—if she hasn't sold them already.''

"I'll be damned," said Gabe, sounding impressed. "That kind of money could be a tempting target all by itself."

"It might even make a plain lady look a little prettier, right? Maybe you're thinking she needs a different man in her life?"

Gabe shot a hard look at Sarah, then laughed when he saw the twinkle in her eyes. "You're just lucky I've got money of my own," he said. "Otherwise I'd still be over there making eyes at her."

"Oh, yeah?" said Sarah. "If you have money of your own then I'm not getting enough of it."

Gabe winked at her and said, "Enough of what?" Then he ducked the pillow she threw at him, laughing as he picked it out of the air and tossed it back. The woman hugged it against her breasts, giving him a look that was full of warmth and mischief at the same time.

"Anyway," she said, "there's just one problem with your theory. If it *was* her money they were after, then it still doesn't explain the deed."

"Unless it was a dodge," said Gabe. "Everyone knew about the bad blood between Haywood and Tomlin, right? So this guy I shot figured he'd get people looking the other way and no one would think of suspecting him."

Sarah shrugged, watching Gabe as he slipped a hand-tooled holster over his shoulder. It held a Remington snugly beneath his right arm, the butt pointing out for a cross draw. Gabe had spent most of a bitter winter learning to shoot with his left hand, to avoid the awkwardness of the trigger finger he'd broken on Stanley Price's jaw. There was also a sheath sewn on the back of the holster that held a Green River knife with its handle hanging down beside the barrel of the revolver. The arrangement let Gabe decide which weapon would be most effective while he was still reaching for them.

"Looks like you're loaded for bear," Sarah teased him. "Where'd you ever find a contraption like that?"

Gabe put on a black broadcloth coat to cover the shoulder rig. "I didn't," he said. "I had it made for me in Boston."

"When you went looking for your mother's family?"

Gabe nodded stiffly and turned toward the door.

"Hey?" said the woman. She had thrown off the covers by the time Gabe turned around again, stretching her long legs and shifting onto her back so she was looking at him over the mounds of her breasts. "Hurry back?"

Gabe gave her a blank look and shook his head, pretending confusion. "Was I going somewhere?"

Sarah laughed and Gabe could still hear the music of her laughter even after he'd closed the door and started walking away.

His smile disappeared when he saw the crowds that lined the street in front of the saloon. It was lunchtime, with the sun high overhead, but storeowners lounged in their doorways, trading gossip with the customers who had gathered in small groups along the boardwalk.

"—bad news," someone was saying.

"For Haywood, maybe. Good news for Thorne."

"That son of a bitch."

"I bet he come in his pants when he had a chance to arrest Mr. Haywood."

"Think he'll try anything?"

"Goddamn better not."

Gabe frowned, matching the talk against Sarah's reaction when he'd told her the story at dawn. She had also been worried for Haywood's safety in the county jail, explaining that Thorne had failed as a rancher and been forced to sell out to Haywood—who he blamed for his failure. Those were the rumors, anyway. What everyone knew for a fact was that the rancher and the sheriff didn't get along. Now the sheriff had Haywood in custody and Gabe wondered if he'd regret his part of it. He looked up the street when four riders appeared around a corner, Haywood and Thorne flanked by two deputies.

A fifth horse trailed along behind with a blanket-wrapped body draped across its back. Gabe thought of the old man he'd killed the night before, seeing in his mind the broken teeth and the vague, watery eyes. He realized he had never learned the man's name, as if it didn't seem important, and now the more Gabe thought about him the more unlikely it seemed that he could have planned everything out by himself. It would have taken nerve as well as imagination to decide what to do and how to do it.

Gabe focused on the rancher with new interest, trying to picture him making those decisions, but it was almost as hard. Frank Haywood was smart enough, all right, but Gabe kept remembering the rancher's bull-headed temper in Tomlin's store—and then the flash of humor that had made it hard not to like him.

Gabe turned his attention to the sheriff, wondering about the enmity between the two men, and had a sudden feeling that they were cut from the same cloth. Both were big men with square jaws and broad, sloping shoulders, but it was more than that: they also had the same look of hard-set, dogged determination in their eyes. Haywood and Thorne never looked at each other as they rode down the street but you could see the struggle brewing between them. Gabe found himself thinking of the way buffalo bulls sometimes sidle toward each other, finally knocking heads if one of them doesn't back off.

And if the bulls are matched too evenly for a quick end to the contest, Gabe knew, it could mean a fight to the death.

The riders passed by and one of the deputies turned off, taking the outlaw's body to the undertaker. Gabe kept his eye on the rancher, who looked straight ahead and refused to acknowledge the people staring at him from the boardwalk. Gabe weaved his way among them, following the procession until it stopped in front of the jail.

Haywood stayed on his horse, contemplating the building, and Gabe looked at it too. It was an ugly squat structure made of cut sandstone blocks. There were iron bars over narrow ground-level windows, indicating basement cells which would be that much harder to blast out of. The only entrance seemed to be a steel-plated door set in the front. Gabe saw the sheriff say something and after a moment the big rancher swung down off his horse. He walked toward the door with the sheriff and the remaining deputy close behind.

Gabe trotted across the street and followed them inside, his boots making a hollow sound across the boardwalk. The sheriff spun on his heel and slapped his holster as Gabe came through the door. The deputy at his side did the same thing, eyeing Gabe suspiciously while a third deputy stood up behind a railing that sectioned off a desk and a couple of gun racks against one wall. Haywood was looking at Gabe over Thorne's shoulder, his expression no more friendly than anyone else's.

"Who the hell are you?" Thorne growled.

Gabe started to say something but Chester Tomlin came rushing in through the open door. The little storekeeper stopped and blinked his eyes in confusion for a moment, peering from Gabe to the sheriff and back again. Then he laughed nervously and said, "It's all right, Harry. This is the fellow I was telling you about."

"Sure," Haywood grunted, "I should've known."

Gabe looked away, then felt surprised that he had. There were three other men in the room but Haywood was the only one who seemed to count—the only one whose opinion meant anything. Gabe forced himself to meet Haywood's stare.

"This is Gabe Conrad," Tomlin was telling Thorne. "He can back up everything I told you about my wife's rescue."

The sheriff was giving Gabe a closer look. "You followed the man who picked up the money?"

Gabe nodded, aware of Haywood watching him just as closely over Thorne's shoulder.

"You never saw anyone else?"

Gabe shook his head.

"Tell us where you found Mrs. Tomlin."

Gabe described the grove of pines, the direction of his travel up the wash, and the cabin at the base of a low hill. When he heard about the cabin, Thorne nodded and gave the rancher an accusing look.

"Jesus Christ!" Haywood exploded, ignoring the nervous deputy standing guard behind him. "I know we ain't exactly friends, Harry, but you can't think I'd be stupid enough to use my own place. I might as well hang out a sign."

"Except you didn't think anyone would find out," said Tomlin. All eyes turned to the storekeeper and his cheeks flushed a bright red. "Don't forget, no one would have known about the cabin if my man hadn't followed your man. You never expected that."

Gabe scowled at the idea that he belonged to anyone, but he was still watching Haywood and now he noticed a thoughtfulness in the rancher's eyes as he studied Chester Tomlin.

"There's also the horses the man used," said Thorne. "I've got 'em at the stable, Frank, and they're wearin' your brand all right."

"I got two hundred horses," Haywood said wearily. "Not

to mention seven thousand head of cattle. And people know they can get away with stealin' anything they want as long as you're the sheriff in this county.''

"The hell with you!'' Thorne yelled, taking a step toward Haywood. "I also have the note telling Mr. Tomlin what to do.''

"I never wrote any note.''

"Don't matter. It just says for Mr. Tomlin to send the deed—*signed over to you*—if he ever wants to see his wife again. I got the deed, too.''

"None of it means a goddamn thing, Harry. Jesus Christ, you're still as dumb as you ever was.''

Thorne slammed the butt plate of his rifle into Haywood's belly. Gabe and the deputies all started moving in—Gabe to stop a beating and the deputies to pitch in—but Haywood only winced and folded a little at the waist, never taking his eyes off the sheriff. Gabe nodded with respect, seeing that the rancher would not let himself be goaded into making stupid mistakes. Gabe also saw the murderous look in his eyes and felt glad it wasn't aimed at him.

Gabe cleared his throat in that instant of tense silence and said, "Maybe the deed really *isn't* the point.''

Now he was the center of attention again. Even the deputy who had gone back to his desk behind the barrier was watching him.

"What the hell are you talking about?'' said Thorne.

"That note asked for a fair amount of money, right? How much was it, Mr. Tomlin?''

"Ten thousand.''

Gabe whistled in spite of himself. "A man could live half the rest of his life on that. See what I mean?''

"No, I don't,'' said the sheriff, hatred still smouldering in his eyes.

"Well suppose you wanted to feel safe while you were spending all that money. Wouldn't you try to make sure the wrong man got arrested?"

The sheriff frowned, glancing at Chester Tomlin. "That's pretty slick thinkin'," he admitted. "Trouble is, the man you killed weren't nothin' but a drifter. I can't see him comin' up with an idea like that."

"Of course not," said Gabe. He nodded at Tomlin and Haywood and said, "Besides, a drifter wouldn't likely know about the fight these two had."

"Exactly," said Thorne, "so why—"

"But that's just the point," said Gabe. "The drifter was hired by someone here in Sidney who *did* know. Someone who also knew that Mr. Tomlin's wife came into a lot of money."

Thorne gave Gabe a suspicious look, then turned to the storekeeper. "Did you tell him about that, Chester?"

Tomlin shook his head and the deputy behind the barrier laughed. "I bet he got it from Sarah Prater," the deputy said, his tone edged with jealousy. "No one else is getting near her these days."

"The point is," Gabe said coldly. "If the wrong man got arrested, then the right one could stay in town and enjoy the money."

Thorne was nodding slowly. "Maybe it wouldn't hurt to ask around," he said. "Find out who the drifter was seen with."

"You won't have to," said Tomlin, lifting his chin a little higher under the pressure of everyone looking at him. "I saw him talking to Mr. Haywood last Wednesday night."

Haywood didn't react. He just kept his green eyes fixed on the storekeeper. But it was enough.

"It's true," Tomlin sputtered, his voice high-pitched and nervous. "That's the same day you came into my shop and manhandled me. Later on I saw the two of you in the alley behind McClary's Cafe.''

The sheriff was looking at Haywood, waiting for a denial, but he kept staring at Tomlin. "I understand," said the rancher, his voice as ominous as it was soft. "I see what you're up to."

The storekeeper met his eyes with a struggle until the sheriff gave him an excuse to look away.

"Will you swear to that?" Thorne asked him.

Tomlin nodded. "He won't get away with abusing my wife."

Thorne was frowning. "But it has to be the truth," he said.

"I know what I saw! You just put me on the stand. And there's one more thing you better think about. If someone was going to use that deed as a decoy, they'd have to know about it first."

Gabe felt a sinking sensation in his stomach.

"Which lets out just about everybody," Tomlin said triumphantly. "Unless you want to accuse the county clerk or the man who sold the property. I kept the sale quiet, so they were the only ones who knew —besides Mr. Haywood."

"Why all the secrecy?" said Gabe.

"You were there. You saw what happened when he found out. That's why he tried to beat me senseless that day." The storekeeper's chin was trembling. "Then that very night I saw him talking to the man who took my wife from our home. And almost violated her on the floor of his line shack."

There was another silence as attention shifted to the rancher. He didn't seem to notice. He kept staring at Tomlin while everyone stared at him, with Gabe feeling an urge to apologize for the way his idea had backfired. It just made him more confused. All his instincts told him that Haywood wasn't guilty of anything, but all the facts and logic said he was.

"Well, I guess that does it," Thorne finally said. "The great Frank Haywood is gonna find himself on the wrong end of a rope."

The rancher swivelled his head on its massive bull neck, eyeing the sheriff without fear. "That would give you a lot of pleasure, wouldn't it?"

"I hope they let me pull the trap, you son of a bitch. Now empty your pockets on the desk." Thorne nodded to the deputy behind the desk. "Bill, go find the dirtiest, smelliest, coldest cell you can find. And you two"—looking at Gabe and Chester Tomlin—"we don't need to keep you here any longer."

Tomlin nodded and looked at Gabe, tilting his head toward the door. "Come on," he said. "Let me buy you some dinner."

But Gabe hesitated, feeling uneasy as he watched the rancher pull things out of his pockets. The deputy named Bill went through a gate behind Haywood and started down the stairs, the clatter of his boots echoing back up into the room. After a moment the sound mingled with a rapid drumming of heels on the boardwalk outside. Gabe looked toward the doorway just as Sam McClure burst through, his eyes burning with fury.

CHAPTER SEVEN

Gabe had to look twice to convince himself that the newcomer was Marshal McClure. The mild, almost sleepy man he remembered was now a man who breathed fire. McClure was still a little old for his job, maybe, and closer in size to Chester Tomlin than to Haywood or Thorne, but the force of his anger made him seem a lot bigger. Gabe could feel it as an urge to step back out of the way.

"So it's true," said McClure, glaring at the sheriff. "Damn it, Harry, I didn't think even you would sink this low."

"I didn't sink nowhere," Thorne blurted. "What the hell are you talking about?"

"Using your badge like this, just to make trouble for an enemy."

"That's what you think, is it?"

"What else could it be?"

"As a matter of fact, McClure, your friend is standing in deep shit." Thorne was making no effort to hide his satisfaction. "We got him dead to rights this time."

"That's impossible. What for?"

"Stealin' Mr. Tomlin's wife, that's what for. Holdin' her against her will and makin' threats against her life."

McClure's head snapped back in surprise. He shot a quick look at Haywood, and Gabe had the feeling that some kind of understanding passed between the two men. McClure calmed down a little, his expression more puzzled than angry. "This is crazy," he told the sheriff. "Frank wouldn't do anything like that and you know it."

"I don't know any such thing. Besides," said Thorne, nodding at Gabe, "we have plenty of proof."

"You!" said the marshal, giving Gabe a dark look. "I should've run you out the first day."

"Now hold on," said Thorne. "Haywood got his ownself in trouble. This fella just caught him at it." Gabe forced himself to meet McClure's cold grey eyes while the sheriff started to list the evidence against Haywood.

"That's a bunch of horseshit!" McClure exploded. "Suppose I steal your horse, Harry, and leave it behind when I kill someone."

"You didn't let me finish. Mr. Tomlin saw Haywood talkin' to the drifter last week."

"So he claims," said McClure.

"Well, what about the deed? You can't deny that Haywood was the only one who knew about it."

"Sure I can." The marshal looked at the storekeeper. "What about the man who *paid* for the property."

"What!" said Tomlin.

Thorne was blinking in confusion. "What're you gettin' at?" he said.

"Let's agree that someone hired the drifter. It didn't have to be Frank."

"Are you tryin' to say . . . you're out of your mind, McClure! Why would Mr. Tomlin do that to his own wife?"

The marshal glanced at Haywood, who moved his head a fraction of an inch to one side. Gabe thought he was the only one who'd seen it and the movement was so slight that he wasn't all that sure of it himself. But McClure scowled impatiently and said, "It's still a bunch of horseshit, Thorne."

"It's enough to make an arrest."

McClure squinted at the sheriff for a moment, chewing the inside of his lip in thoughtful concentration. There was a pounding of heels in the stairwell and a moment later the deputy named Bill came through the door that led to the cells. When he saw the marshal he took up a position near the back of the room, standing off to one side with a wary look.

"Is Judge Wilcox still in Washington?" McClure asked the sheriff.

"Due back in four days."

McClure frowned, scratching the side of his neck. "Then I guess it'll be up to him—"

"Damn right," said Thorne.

"—but in the meantime I'm taking custody of the prisoner."

"The hell you are!" the sheriff roared. "I went out and got him and he belongs to me."

"But Mrs. Tomlin was abducted within the city limits," McClure said as he moved toward the rancher. "That's my jurisdiction and my responsibility."

Thorne jumped in front of him, gripping the butt of his pistol when McClure kept coming. "Stay where you are, damn you."

The marshal didn't stop until he was standing directly in front of Thorne, staring up into his face with unblinking eyes. "Get out of the way," he said.

"Do you think I'm stupid, McClure? If I turn Frank over to you he'll disappear and that'll be the end of it."

The marshal rocked forward on the balls of his feet. "I oughta knock you down for that!"

"Try it, little man. Haywood stays here."

"Where you can get at him whenever you feel like it."

"I won't need to. A jury is gonna convict your friend and then I'm gonna hang him by the neck until he's dead."

"He'll never make it to trial," said McClure. "Not in your custody. I'm taking him with me."

"Don't try it," the sheriff warned. He tilted his head toward the deputy guarding Haywood and the second deputy at the back of the room. "We've got you flanked and by God we'll kill you if you start anything. The federal courts'll back us up."

The two lawmen stood toe to toe, one towering over the other and neither one of them ready to give an inch. Gabe wasn't sure what was going to happen but the marshal didn't look like a man who was worrying about the odds. Gabe shifted his balance a little, ready to jump in if McClure started things rolling. He didn't see anything wrong with that since Thorne hadn't had the balls to face the marshal man to man. So Gabe kept a close eye on McClure's shoulders for the first hint of movement, deciding to concentrate on Thorne's deputies with his first shots. He had a feeling the marshal could take care of Thorne by himself.

Then the rancher let out a long sigh and shook his head.

"Don't do it," he told McClure. "There's other ways to fight this. In the meantime I need you alive."

It looked as if backing down would be about as easy for the marshal as getting back to the edge of a cliff after you've jumped off. But gradually the tension went out of his body until you could see him breathing again.

"You'll have it your way for now," he said, his voice as

taught as a piano wire. "But you better take good care of your prisoner."

"Who do you think—"

"Shut up and listen, Thorne! Frank Haywood comes out of here alive or I kill you myself."

"You can't talk to me that way!"

"I just did," said McClure, leaning forward again with his forehead only a few inches from the sheriff's chin. "You called me a little man but now I'm calling your bluff and I don't see you doing anything about it. What does that make you?"

Thorne clenched his fists at his sides and looked down at the marshal with a furious hatred. The ridge of his jaw stood out in a hard line and again Gabe thought there would be a fight. Then the sheriff's eyes flickered and Gabe knew he could relax.

"I ain't gonna bother myself," the sheriff said. "I'll just let you stew about your friend bein' in my custody."

"You won't get the satisfaction, Thorne. Just remember what I said."

"Get the hell out of here, McClure."

The marshal lingered a moment longer to make it clear that he was leaving by choice. Then he glanced once more at Haywood before he made a show of strolling casually out of the jail. Thorne watched the door for several seconds after he left, then looked at the rancher. Something in his eyes put a cold chill next to Gabe's heart.

"OK," the sheriff said to his deputies. "Take the bastard downstairs. If he gives you any trouble, give it right back to him."

Gabe was already halfway to the door, brushing by the storekeeper in his hurry to leave. He heard Tomlin say his name but he kept going.

"Hey!" the sheriff yelled after him. "Get your ass back here."

But Gabe was outside and cutting across the street, blinking against the bright sun as he called out to McClure. The marshal stopped on the other side and waited for him in the shade of an awning, making no effort to speak after Gabe caught up with him. For his part Gabe didn't waste time with apologies or explanations.

"You have some good men working for you?" he asked.

"One less than I had a week ago."

"I hope the others are smarter," Gabe flared. "Would one or two of them be loyal to Mr. Haywood?"

"That describes just about everybody in town, mister. When they hear about your—"

"Then maybe it wouldn't be too hard to post someone outside the jail. Day and night until the trial."

McClure shoved his hands in his pockets, his gaze drifting thoughtfully to the stone building he'd just left.

"That way," said Gabe, "Haywood could let out a yell if—"

"I understand," McClure snapped. "I'm not dense."

"I know, sir."

That brought the marshal's attention back to Gabe. "There's something I *don't* understand," he said. "I thought you were on their side."

"I thought I was helping Mrs. Tomlin."

"Then why all this concern for the man who's accused of abducting her."

"You don't believe it, do you? I'm not sure I do either."

"But even so," said the marshal, "why come to me? You don't have any stake in this."

Gabe looked surprised. "Of course I do. If Mr. Haywood is innocent and something happens to him . . . well, I wouldn't want any part of that."

McClure nodded but his expression remained skeptical. He studied Gabe like a chess player trying to understand an opponent's latest move.

"Look," Gabe said impatiently, "you know it's a good idea and I know you'll follow up on it. That's all that matters, all right?"

"But I still don't understand—"

"You don't have to."

Gabe turned away, eager to get back to Sarah, but he noticed Chester Tomlin standing in front of the jail. The storekeeper was shading his eyes and looking across the street, as if he'd been watching all along. When he saw Gabe looking back at him he dropped his hand and started across the street.

"I don't know your game," McClure murmured behind Gabe. "But watch out for that character."

Gabe heard the marshal moving off along the boardwalk while Tomlin scurried across the street, dodging horses and freight wagons that were kicking up great clouds of dust. The dust-filled air glowed orange in the bright sun.

"What was all that about?" Tomlin said when he came up to Gabe. "What kind of business did you have with McClure?"

"I guess that's between him and me, isn't it?"

The storekeeper held up his hands. "Sorry," he said. "No offense meant. It's just that Thorne wasn't happy about you running off like that."

"The sheriff's happiness doesn't mean much to me."

"Jesus Christ, Gabe, what's got into you?"

"I don't like being treated like a hired hand, Tomlin. I did you a favor but that doesn't make me 'your man.' Understand that?"

"I do, my friend. I understand perfectly. I wanted to bite

my tongue as soon as I said it. I hope you'll accept my invitation to luncheon by way of an apology.''

"That's not necessary.''

"But I want to.'' He looked down as if he was embarrassed. "In fact, I have an ulterior motive. There's another proposition I want to discuss.''

"You'd be wasting your time,'' said Gabe. He started to walk away but Tomlin put a hand on his arm.

"It's not for me, Gabe. Another thing I understand is that you never really did anything for me. You did it for my wife, right? Because she was a woman who needed help.''

Gabe didn't say anything but he realized that Chester Tomlin was more clever than he'd thought.

"All I ask is that you hear me out,'' Tomlin urged. "It won't cost you anything but an hour of your time, whiled away in a cool restaurant that serves an excellent meal.''

Gabe nearly walked away without another word, feeling a powerful and instinctive desire to avoid Chester Tomlin, but his curiosity had been aroused by the hint of concern for Tomlin's wife. As Gabe hesitated, a new thought shifted the balance. Perhaps he would be able to learn something more—and something useful—about the strange events of the last few days.

"As you might have guessed,'' said the storekeeper. "I'm still afraid for my wife's safety. I'm asking you to help me protect her.''

Gabe continued chewing for a moment, savoring the roast pheasant that Tomlin had insisted they order. He had to admit that it was a good choice, as well as a fine restaurant. He was tasting spices that usually didn't get this far west, and he had to force himself to concentrate on his answer to Tomlin's proposition.

"Protection from what?'' he finally said. "You're sure

Haywood's the man responsible, right? And he's in jail now.''

"He's still got friends, though. He'll talk to them. He might even get a lawyer to relay instructions.''

"But I can't imagine—''

"Don't be naive, Gabe! He has twice the reason now. I've still got the land he wants, and now my testimony can hang him. What better way to get at me than through Jane.''

Gabe squirmed in his chair.

"Please?'' said Tomlin. "I'm begging you. It would only be for a couple weeks at the most, until the trial. I'd rest a lot easier knowing Jane is safe.''

"I'm sure she will be,'' Gabe said. "I might as well tell you that I'm not all that sure of Haywood's guilt, for one thing.''

"You're not?'' said Tomlin, looking disturbed.

Gabe shook his head. "And even if he is, he'd be a fool to make things worse by—''

"But what if you're wrong, Gabe? Even if there's a *chance* you're wrong. How would you feel if something happened to Jane?''

Gabe shifted position again, looking uncomfortable. "There are a lot of men around,'' he said. "And plenty of 'em are looking for jobs.''

"Not one of them has a tenth of your natural abilities. You've already proven that. I want to feel secure, Gabe. I want to *know* my wife is safe.''

"And I'm convinced she is.''

"Then I'll just repeat my question. Suppose you're wrong? Suppose I hire some other . . . some drifter who makes a mistake. How will you feel when you learn that Jane has been ravished or perhaps even killed?''

Gabe scowled and looked away.

"I don't know whether you had an opportunity to become

acquainted,'' Tomlin pressed, ''but she's a good, kind woman. She deserves to be protected.''

Gabe nodded, still frowning.

''Don't you believe it's better to be safe than sorry?''

''Of course,'' said Gabe.

''I'm not asking all that much, you know. All you'd have to do is stay in our home for a week or two, with your own room. You'd take meals with us. You'd accompany my wife on her errands. How can you refuse me?''

Gabe sighed. ''I guess that's the problem,'' he said. ''I can't.''

CHAPTER EIGHT

Gabe came out of the same restaurant the next afternoon and held the door open while he studied the street. No one paid him any special attention as far as he could tell, nor was anyone loitering nearby. He looked back through the doorway and nodded his head, and a moment later Jane Tomlin followed him outside. She wore a long plain dress in a lighter shade of brown than the one he'd seen before, and clutched a brown suede handbag beneath her breasts. A matching sun bonnet covered most of her hair, which was also brown and somewhat faded. She stood before him in the shade for a moment, gazing down the street with a far-away look in her eye.

"What's the next stop?" Gabe asked.

"I don't know."

"Perhaps you'd prefer to go home?"

Jane Tomlin peered into Gabe's face as if she was searching for a hidden meaning. She'd been doing that a lot since her husband had announced his agreement with Gabe the day before. Instead of appearing relieved, or even a little annoyed at the intrusion into her daily routine, she had accepted Gabe's assignment with a downcast resignation that left him puzzled. Several times he had caught her watching him intently, but his efforts to engage her in conversation had been rewarded with no more than a dozen spoken words during their long hours together.

In short, her behavior was making no more sense than anything else Gabe had experienced in Sidney. He still didn't know whether Frank Haywood could truly be guilty of planning Jane Tomlin's abduction. And if he wasn't, then Gabe was no closer to knowing who had made it look that way—and why. As for the woman, why did she refuse to speak? Why did she regard him with such suspicion and carry herself with such a heavy air of defeat? It was clear to Gabe that some part of the story remained hidden. He feared that his failure to uncover it was exposing him to danger. He knew with an increasing sense of urgency that he would have to keep looking.

The woman interrupted his thoughts with a long and heavy sigh. "Let's just walk a while," she said, adjusting her bonnet and smoothing her hair. "I like to see the town when it's this busy."

She walked away and Gabe caught up, falling in beside her.

"If that's the case," he said, "I have some business I'd like to attend to."

"Whatever you say."

"Maybe you can help. Do you know who keeps the records on property sales in this county?"

"Tom Haskins does. The county clerk."

"Better yet, did your husband ever mention the name of the man who sold him that quarter section with the lake?"

The woman gave him a sideways glance. "Why?" she asked.

"Tell me something first. Do you still have a hard time believing that they have the right man locked up?"

Jane Tomlin glanced down the street toward the jail, then stopped to face Gabe with that searching look of hers. Her features were drawn and haggard and possibly touched with fear. "I'm not acquainted with Mr. Haywood on a personal basis," she said. "But people do speak highly of him."

"That's what I keep hearing, and it goes along with the feeling I had about him myself. I don't mean anything against Mr. Tomlin, ma'am, but I want to find out more about what's happening here. Starting with that deed."

"What do you want to know?"

"Anything and everything," Gabe said with a shrug. "It seems like the worst piece of evidence against Haywood, but I keep wondering why your husband owned the land in the first place."

Jane Tomlin nodded thoughtfully, still watching him. "I can't answer that," she said. "But I know he bought it a little more than two weeks ago from a man named Wayne Minter."

"Two weeks!" said Gabe. "Is Minter local?"

"He still has his farm. It's about three miles east."

"I can't leave you alone," Gabe said with a frown. "Would you be willing to ride out with me if I rented a buggy?"

"I suppose," she said, giving him that look again. "Yes. I would."

The livery offered a one-horse carriage with a roof to shield them from the sun that was blazing down from a cloudless sky. There were also a couple of linen dusters under the seat to keep the worst of the dirt off their clothes. Gabe took the main road to the east, following the railroad tracks for a time and letting his mind wander when the woman fell into her customary silence. Almost an hour later she looked at him and then pointed into the distance.

Gabe nodded, turning onto a path that led to a ramshackle farmyard. The buggy lurched and swayed in the ruts and for a moment he and Jane Tomlin were thrown together, their shoulders touching long enough for him to feel her warmth. They looked at each other and Gabe suddenly remembered the soft, full curves of her body in the cabin in the lamplight. He had come to think of her as a worn-out and sexless woman, but now he felt as if he'd caught a hint of something still alive deep inside. His blood began to race and he was so surprised that he stared at the woman longer than he should have. A frightened look came into her eyes and she turned away.

Chickens squawked and fluttered off on all sides as Gabe guided the buggy toward a water trough beneath a windmill in the center of the yard. A one-room shack stood on the right, facing a much larger barn on the left. There was hay in the barn and two milk cows in an attached corral, and six or seven hogs in a long shed behind the corral. The hogs were clustered around a tall, stringy man who was dumping a pail of scraps.

Gabe pulled on the reins and a cloud of dust settled over the buggy as it came to a stop in front of the trough. The horse plunged its snout into the water while the squealing and grunting of hogs drifted across the yard. The stringy man stopped what he was doing to watch the buggy. Gabe looked at the woman for confirmation. She nodded without meeting his eyes.

"Maybe it'd be better if you wait here," he suggested as he tied off the reins. "Minter might talk easier if it's just me. Besides, you'll have the shade."

Jane Tomlin nodded again and Gabe got out of the buggy,

stepping carefully through a yard covered with dung heaps. His first impression was that Wayne Minter didn't take good care of his farm. Or himself, for that matter. Minter's long skinny neck was grimy with dirt and his clothes were nearly shredded. He set the pail down in the slop and watched Gabe approach with a mean and sullen look on his face.

"What the hell do you want?" he said.

Gabe's eyes turned cool. "What do I want?" he echoed. "Some polite behavior would be a good place to start."

"Fuck you!" said Minter. "Get off my farm."

He started to push Gabe back toward the carriage but Gabe grabbed one bony wrist to restrain him. The farmer tried to hit him with his other hand so Gabe caught that wrist, too, twisting his arms back. Minter continued to struggle until Gabe forced him to his knees in the slop. The pigs surrounded them, grunting and rooting around.

"What's going on?" Gabe said. "Do you always treat strangers this way?"

"Shit, you ain't no stranger. Let go of my arms."

"You ready to behave yourself?"

"I'd kill you if I could," Minter said sullenly. "But I ain't a man to take stupid chances."

Gabe released his grip and stepped back a foot or two, giving the farmer a closer look as he got to his feet. "I don't place you," said Gabe. "You really think you know me?"

Minter pointed his chin toward the buggy. "I know Jane Tomlin, don't I? So it has to be that bastard husband of hers that sent you out here."

"Now I'm really confused," said Gabe. "You're not feeling all that friendly toward Chester Tomlin, is that it?"

"I don't care if he knows it, either. Tell him I said he can go fuck himself."

"But if you feel that way, why'd you do business with the man?"

"Business! We didn't do no business. It was more like a rape. The bastard fucked me over."

"You didn't want to sell that land?"

"Not to him, anyway. That piece was part of my original homestead and I chose it well. I knew it'd be worth a lot of money if I ever decided to quit ranchin' and go to farmin'." Minter looked at the buggy again, then frowned at Gabe. "You sayin' you really don't know 'bout this?"

"I'm trying to protect the woman," said Gabe. "That's all."

"So what're you doin' out here?"

"I can protect her better if I know what's going on. You decided to sell after all?"

"Hell, I never did like cows. I wanted to spend my time here. I had a real fine offer, too—plenty of money to fix things up and maybe hire some help. Tomlin only gave me half as much."

"Then why did you sell it to him?"

Minter gazed toward his house and barn. The windmill started to turn in a fresh breeze and the sucker rods rubbed against the standpipe, giving off a squealing, plaintive moan. "I know this ain't much of a place," he said, "but it's all I got."

"You mean Tomlin threatened to take it away?"

The farmer nodded. "Said he could have my note called due. I'd have to let 'em take the place."

"That'd be the bank?" said Gabe. "How could he get the bank to do that?"

The farmer shrugged. "I think he owns it or something."

"You're sure about that?"

"The little bastard ain't exactly what he looks like, you know."

"I guess not."

"He didn't even buy the land in his own name. Had me make the title out to something called the Sidney Development Company."

"Well, well," said Gabe. "He's full of surprises, isn't he?"

"You can say that again." Minter was staring at his feet, his thin shoulders drooping lower and lower. "I just hope I ain't got myself in even worse trouble with him."

"How?"

"Aw, you know. Getting hot and blowing off like that." He looked up at Gabe with deep-set, hollow eyes. "If I lose this place I might as well just hang myself."

"Don't worry," said Gabe. "None of it'll get back to Tomlin."

"I'd 'preciate it. I'm sorry about—"

"Forget it. Can't say as I blame you, from what I've heard. But one more question about that offer. Was it Frank Haywood who made it?"

Minter looked surprised. "That's right," he said. "How'd you know?"

"And he found out what happened last week sometime?"

"That's right! He came by on Wednesday and I had to tell him. Sure hated to do it. But how did you—what's going on here?"

"I wish I knew," Gabe said with a scowl. "But it looks like I stopped a fight when I should've let it go." He told the farmer about his run-in with Haywood, followed by Jane Tomlin's abduction the next week, and Haywood's arrest. "But what would Tomlin want with that property, anyway?" Gabe finally asked. "Did he say? Can you see him running cows?"

The farmer laughed and said, "Brother, tell me another one."

"I hope I can," said Gabe, looking thoughtful. "Maybe I should go and have that talk with the county clerk."

Jane Tomlin still hadn't said anything by the time they were halfway back to Sidney. Gabe tried again, asking about the Sidney Development Company and any reason her husband might have for buying Minter's land. But she simply shrugged and stared straight ahead, clutching her handbag in her lap.

"Why all the silence?" he snapped at her. "You're not being much help, Mrs. Tomlin."

She gave him a startled look and began to scratch the side of her head. Slowly she moved her fingers higher and higher until she decided to take her sun bonnet off altogether, holding it in one hand while she smoothed her dust-matted hair with the other. Then one of the wheels hit a rock and the bonnet went flying out of her hand.

Gabe yanked back on the reins, trying to hide his irritation but taking it out on the horses. "Don't worry," he said, jumping down. "I'll get it." He was vaguely aware of the woman watching him as he walked back to retrieve her bonnet, and he wondered why she couldn't even thank him for his efforts. It was just one more thing he didn't understand. He felt himself getting madder and more frustrated by the moment. He was bending over to pick the bonnet out of the dirt, thinking of everything he wanted to say to the woman, when he heard her yell something. Then he heard the slap of reins and the rattle of wheels as the buggy rolled away.

Gabe spun around and broke into a run almost before he knew what he was doing. His reaction probably made the difference. Jane Tomlin was lashing frantically at the pony, but it was so used to a light trotting pace that it didn't understand at first what she wanted. Gabe started gaining on the carriage. The woman threw frightened looks over her shoulder and snapped the reins as hard as she could, screaming at the horse. It started moving faster and Gabe pumped his legs that much harder. He felt the wind in his hair just as he had felt it as a boy, during the endless foot races he had run against the Oglala boys he grew up with.

The pony broke into a real gallop just as Gabe came up behind the carriage. He managed to hold even for a second or two, then threw himself toward the back panel and wrapped his arms over the top. For a moment he was content just to hold on and suck air into his burning lungs. But when he looked up again Jane Tomlin was trying to watch the road while she fumbled with her handbag on the seat beside her.

With a desperate rush of fear Gabe swung himself up and into the carriage. The woman's hand came out of her purse holding a small pistol. She was turning it towards Gabe's chest when he clamped down on her arm. She screamed and tried to break free while Gabe twisted the gun from her hand. Then he wrestled the reins from her other hand. The woman was screaming louder, clawing at his face and trying to get her pistol back as Gabe fought to control the frightened horse. They covered another half-mile before the buggy began to slow down.

But the woman leaped out while the carriage was still moving. She rolled in the dirt and got up and started running through the grass, holding her dress high up around her thighs. Gabe cursed and turned the pony off the road, which was finally enough to get it stopped. He jumped down and ran after the woman. She looked back and screamed and ran faster. Then she tumbled into the grass and didn't get up. When Gabe reached her she was still sprawled on the ground, crying hopelessly and looking up at him with stricken eyes.

"What are you waiting for?" she wailed. "Get it over with, damn you!"

Gabe frowned and shook his head, feeling stupid.

"I can't stand the waiting," she shrieked. "Just kill me and get it over with."

Gabe stood over her with his mouth hanging open.

"Oh, please dear God don't make me beg you."

Jane Tomlin put her hands over her face and sobbed brokenly. Gabe knelt beside her in the grass, tormented by her anguish as if it was his own.

"You're wrong," he said, his tone pleading with her to believe him. "No one will hurt you as long as I'm with you." He touched her arm but she jerked violently away. "I'm sorry I did that, Mrs. Tomlin. I swear I'm not here to harm you."

"I saw it," she said from behind her hands. "Don't tell me, I saw it."

"Saw what?"

"The way you looked at me in the carriage."

Gabe felt as if his head was reeling. "You mean when our shoulders touched?" he said. "I only looked at you that way because you are an attractive woman, nothing more."

"I'll bet! What about what you did to poor old Mr. Minter."

"Well I *am* sorry you saw that," said Gabe, his cheeks burning. "But it was just a misunderstanding, ma'am. He thought—"Gabe's tone was suddenly angry. "As a matter of fact, Mrs. Tomlin, he thought I was working for your husband. *That's* why he was so unfriendly."

The woman opened her fingers far enough to peek up at him. "Well you do, don't you?"

"I don't belong to anyone, damn it. I do what I want."

"But what about the store? The fight you had . . ."

Gabe's eyes rolled up toward the sky. "Seems like I'm gonna answer for that the rest of my life," he said. "But it was nothing more than being in the wrong place at the wrong time. It looked like your husband needed help."

"But you came after me when—"

"When your husband said *you* might be in trouble. I promise, Mrs. Tomlin, I'm here to help you. Not to hurt you."

She stared up at him for a long time, her sobs gradually subsiding. Eventually she wiped some of the tears from her eyes and sat up, sniffing loudly. Then she blushed and looked toward the carriage. "I have a handkerchief in my bag . . ."

Gabe gave her a wry look. "Any more guns?"

"Don't!" the woman pleaded. "I'll look foolish enough as it is if you're telling the truth."

"I am and you don't," Gabe assured her. He helped her to her feet and they walked through the tall yellow grass.

"I felt so hopeless," she said.

"You really believed I was planning to kill you?"

The woman nodded and Gabe frowned in thought.

"And you believed I was working for your husband," he said. "Is that right?"

Jane Tomlin nodded again.

"But why would he hire me to protect you in the first place?"

"To make it look better. So no one would think he was behind it."

"And yet you do."

The woman nodded a third time, staring at the ground as they walked.

"Why?" said Gabe. "What makes you think he wants to harm you?"

She gave him the familiar searching look, then turned

away. She clearly didn't trust him yet, or at least she didn't trust him with everything. He tried to see it from her side, how everything must have appeared.

"I've heard the rumors," he said after a moment. "I mean the ones about you inheriting a lot of money. That's the only reason I can think of."

She glanced at him again but her eyes were still veiled, hiding her thoughts.

"But that doesn't figure," said Gabe, feeling frustrated. "Doesn't the money wind up belonging to both of you anyway? I mean, as long as you're married he can do whatever he wants with it, right?"

This time, Jane Tomlin looked at him as if to say: you *really* don't know? And in that instant he did.

"That's it, isn't it?" he said. "You're planning to leave him."

The woman looked down quickly and didn't take her eyes off the ground.

"Sure," said Gabe. "It looks like your husband has big plans. He's sure working on a lot more than owning one hardware store. So he needs your money, right?" Gabe nodded thoughtfully. "Of course. And just think how he'd feel if he found out you weren't planning on staying married to him."

Jane Tomlin still didn't say anything and for an instant Gabe had doubts, thinking of the meek, nervous little storekeeper he had first seen behind the counter. Then the woman glanced at him once more. It was only for a second but it was long enough for Gabe to see the flutter of fear in her eyes.

That was all he needed to see.

CHAPTER NINE

The sun was casting long shadows across the streets of Sidney when Gabe escorted Jane Tomlin into her husband's store. All they saw at first were two burly men in front of a display case. Then they heard a familiar voice.

"—betting Winchester will be *the* name in rifles," Tomlin was saying. "Look here. This is a steel frame, my friend. Not brass. This weapon takes a lot of punishment and keeps on shooting."

Gabe allowed himself the ghost of a smile. It was gone by the time Tomlin handed the carbine to the two men for inspection and looked around them to see who had come in the door.

"Jane!" he said. "I'm glad you came by. Hello, Gabe. Can you stay a few minutes?"

The woman nodded solemnly and began to stroll through the store, looking at tools and tin sheeting and rolls of wire while her husband talked to his customers. Sometimes she frowned and touched things out of curiosity, like a windmill rod-puller or a posthole digger. Her husband watched her with a puzzled frown, telling Gabe that this was a new interest of hers.

The customers bought a Winchester apiece and five hundred rounds of ammunition between them. Gabe's eyebrows shot up in surprise and he listened more closely. The men had come out from Philadelphia, they said. They planned to make a big strike in the Black Hills and go home with pockets full of money. But they had been hearing stories about "them goddamn Sioux," so they were preparing themselves for the threat.

"Not that they scare us," said one of the men. "Shit, them redskins'll be sorry if they try anything."

Gabe noticed that the men were wearing black coats and black hats. Funeral colors. He thought that was about right. Chester Tomlin took their money and sent them on their way with a thin-lipped grin, wiping the sheen of perspiration off his forehead. Then he locked the door and pulled the shades and put a "closed" sign in the window. When he turned around again he wasn't smiling. He glanced from his wife to Gabe and back again.

"I trust it's been a good day?" he said. "No incidents so far?"

Gabe looked at the woman, who looked at her husband and shook her head.

"The reason I ask," said Tomlin, "someone saw the two of you leaving town in a rented carriage."

"It was a pleasant day for a drive," said the woman.

"Sure," said Gabe. "Besides, it's easier to keep track of things out on the prairie. You can see what's coming at you."

Tomlin studied them with a speculative look. "Even so, I must say I was surprised. I heard you went east."

"That's true," Gabe said casually. "Wayne Minter lives out that way."

The storekeeper threw a hard look at his wife. "Did you stop to see him?"

Gabe nodded and Jane said, "Uh-huh."

"Am I supposed to drag it out of you?" Tomlin snapped. "Why did you go there? What did he say?"

Gabe had to admit he was enjoying himself. He shrugged and said, "It was nothing, Mr. Tomlin. I just wanted to find out more about that property and why you owned it."

"That's no business of yours."

"No? Even when the deed might be used to hang Frank Haywood?"

"The son of a bitch deserves it!" Tomlin studied his wife for a moment, then turned back to Gabe. "I suppose that lout of a farmer told you a bunch of lies."

"Did he?" said Gabe, letting his eyes get wide. "He seemed to think you were a fine, upstanding businessman."

Tomlin stared at him, feeling certain that he was being toyed with but not sure what to do about it.

"But the thing is," Gabe continued, "I started wondering what else you've been buying."

"With my money," Jane Tomlin put in.

The storekeeper gave her a hurt look. "I thought it was *our* money, dear. I thought you trusted me to make wise investments."

"It looks like you've done just that," said Gabe. "I mean, as long as the town of Sidney stays in business so will you."

"Well, now," said Tomlin, "you might be overstating things a bit . . ."

"Oh?" said Gabe. "You mean you'd rather be modest about your success? Maybe that's why your name doesn't appear on any of the purchases."

"What purchases? What are you talking about?"

"The ones made by the Sidney Development Company, Chester. It's been pretty active these past few months."

"Sidney Development Company? What does that have to do with me?"

"You're saying you never heard of it?"

"Well . . ."

"Because that would make me pretty disappointed in you, Chester. Because the company is owned by the Western Lands Corporation. Have you heard of it?"

Tomlin's lips compressed into a tight line but he didn't say anything.

"Well, I hope so," said Gabe. "Because you're the only stockholder. At first I wasn't sure who to congratulate for all those good investments, but Tom Haskins knew which records to check. He's the county clerk and he's—"

"I know who he is, damn it! You mean to tell me you've been prying into my private affairs?"

Gabe shrugged. "It was hot outside and his office was nice and cool."

"It's no joke," Tomlin yelled. "I will not tolerate this kind of behavior."

"But I thought you'd want people to know. I know *I'd* be proud of owning all the stock in a company that owns the newspaper, two of the best hotels, a saloon. What have I left out? Oh, yeah, the bank!"

"This is crazy!" said the storekeeper. "I hire you for a job and the first thing you do is violate my privacy!"

"No one hires me," said Gabe, staring at Tomlin. "You asked me to protect your wife and I agreed."

"Well, then *do* it, man. Don't expose her to even greater danger with all this foolishness."

Gabe kept staring at Tomlin, his eyes cool and unblinking. "Now you're telling me what to do?" he said.

"Why, you insolent son of a bitch," said the storekeeper. "I'm telling you you're fired, that's what I'm telling you."

"I guess not," said Gabe.

"What!"

"It's one advantage of not working for people. You don't have to stop."

Tomlin's eyes opened wide and his face flushed a bright cherry red. "You'll do as I say, you no-account drifter. Get the hell out of here."

Gabe shook his head and looked at Jane Tomlin. "That isn't your decision, Chester. It's hers."

"Tell this man to leave," Tomlin ordered his wife. "Tell him we don't need him anymore."

The woman could only shake her head, glancing from Tomlin to Gabe with a look of nervous defiance in her dark brown eyes.

Tomlin turned back to Gabe. "What is this? What have you done to Jane?"

"Nothing at all," said Gabe, eyeing the storekeeper with a pointed look. "But I'd say she's still afraid of something."

"Then I'll take care of her myself, if it comes to that. I'm ordering you to get out of my store."

"If you say so." Gabe shrugged and looked at Jane Tomlin. "Are you ready to go?"

"She stays here!" the storekeeper sputtered. "*You're* the one who's going."

"Sorry," said Gabe. "Wherever your wife happens to be, so will I."

"I'll have you arrested."

"For what?"

"I'll . . . I'll have Sheriff Thorne throw you out of the house."

"Don't worry," Gabe said to the woman. "We can always get a couple of rooms at the hotel."

"Not at *my* hotel," Tomlin almost shrieked. "I'll tell them not to let you register."

"Oh, yeah," said Gabe, suppressing a smile, "I forgot you owned it. I guess we'll just have to leave town."

The storekeeper opened his mouth but nothing came out except for a sound that was like a squeak and a grunt at the same time. There was a comical look of helpless disbelief in his eyes, but behind that Gabe could see him thinking furiously, looking for an edge and gradually accepting the fact that there was nothing he could do. He closed his mouth after a while and started breathing better. Then he mopped his face with a handkerchief and put it away, looking at the floor.

"Well," he said. He cleared his throat and peered at Gabe from under his eyebrows. "Please let me apologize for that display," he went on. "I'm quite embarrassed. It's just that I've been worried all day, you see. And then there was the shock of finding out that you'd been digging into my private business affairs. But I'm sure you haven't talked about them with anyone else . . ."

Tomlin looked at Gabe and he shook his head.

"And of course I can expect you to *keep* them private . . ."

This time Gabe only met Tomlin's gaze with a level stare.

The storekeeper frowned and said, "Well, anyway, nothing has changed. I still fear for Jane's safety. I hope we can forget this happened."

"I don't know about forgetting—"

"Put it aside, at least," Tomlin said hastily. "After all, Jane's safety is the important thing."

Gabe's lips twitched a little at the corners. "That's true," he said.

"Wonderful," said Tomlin. "I'm glad we agree." He was extracting a long pigskin wallet from inside his coat. "In fact, let me try to make it up to you. Why don't you and Jane go out and find the best meal there is in Sidney.''

Gabe took the money while Jane Tomlin came a step closer to her husband. ''You'll join us, won't you?'' she said. ''We can wait, if it's just a matter of closing up.''

The storekeeper shook his head. ''I wish I could, dear, but I have some other things to attend to.'' He started walking them toward the door, giving Gabe a conspiratorial smile. ''Now that the cat's out of the bag I guess you can understand. Juggling so many business ventures can keep a man busy.''

Gabe smiled as he left, but it didn't mean what Tomlin thought it meant. *I bet it can,* Gabe thought.

Gabe lay awake far into the night, filling the long and quiet hours with concentrated thought. He thought everything through and then he started over at the beginning, trying to find new ways to look at it. He could not afford to miss a single detail.

One possibility was that nothing else would happen. If an unknown person had arranged the abduction of Jane Tomlin, then he or she could relax now that Frank Haywood was in jail. Or, less likely, it was Haywood who had in fact made the arrangements, but had decided not to take any more chances.

Gabe didn't waste much time thinking along these lines. He was trying to prepare himself for things that *might* happen. The unknown person might take extra precautions, for example, hoping to make sure of Haywood's conviction. Or if Haywood was the culprit, then he might try to force Tomlin to withdraw his testimony.

A final possibility was that Jane Tomlin had been right in believing her husband wanted to harm her. If so, then Gabe expected something to happen fast. He felt sure he had forced Chester Tomlin's hand by discovering his efforts to amass wealth and power in Sidney without letting anyone know. The storekeeper probably wanted to keep it quiet until he was sure that no one could oppose him. Whatever the reason, he might try to make sure that Gabe could never tell anyone else what he'd learned in the county clerk's office.

A soft rasp of sound floated up from somewhere in the house. Gabe held his breath for a moment but he didn't hear it again. Nor did he hear anything in the hall outside his room. The door to the Tomlins' bedroom was fifteen feet away.

If Jane Tomlin was right, in other words, it meant that she would not be the only target. Gabe thought about that as he lay on his bed, fully dressed and listening for any hint of trouble down the hall. It was the reason he had also covered himself with a blanket, ready to fake sleep if someone opened his door. He lay very still, his eyes half-closed as he separated sounds inside the house from those that came through the closed window—the distant rattle of a wagon or the barking of a dog. And he kept reminding himself that there was one more thing to consider: a clever killer might reduce his risk by staying outside Gabe's room and waiting for him to answer some kind of alarm.

All of this was the product of habits so old that Gabe wasn't aware of them any more. It was second nature to think things through with such precision that he could avoid most surprises. He had already tucked his spare Remington inside his belt and packed his belongings into the old warbag beside his bed.

Gabe's eyelids started to droop sometime after one o'clock. A deep and peaceful silence had fallen over the town by then, and Gabe had considered his plans so thoroughly that there was no longer any stimulation in reviewing them. The warm pull of sleep began to get stronger. Gabe fought it by remembering the night that taught him his habit of caution.

It was the night of his release from the stockade at Fort Laramie, a few months after the end of the Civil War. He had been locked up nearly three years for attacking Captain Price. It was Price who had him set free, but Gabe was still a boy and he didn't ask himself how likely it was that the captain had had a change of heart. He didn't *think*. And so he let himself be surprised by three men as he came out of the wash house. They overpowered him and dragged him into a stable, where Price was waiting for a more satisfying form of revenge. The men boxed Gabe in while the captain tried to kill him with a pitchfork.

Gabe could almost see the sputtering lamplight, almost smell the hay and the horseshit. He remembered the vicious grin on the captain's face as he sparred with the pitchfork. He remembered how the prong felt as it speared his palm, scraping against bone and cartilage as the full length went—

Boots pounded in the hall and then the sound was buried in a sudden crash. Gabe was already throwing off the covers when he heard Jane Tomlin scream. He slipped his Remington from under his broadcloth coat and ran to the door, his moccasins making no sound on the hardwood floor. He stood off to one side and threw the door open. An instant later he poked his head into the hall and pulled it back in one sweep of movement, just ahead of two explosions. Bullets splintered the doorframe in front of Gabe's eyes. He blinked but he felt no fear. There was only a cold clarity in his mind and body. It let him keep a precise picture of the two men aiming rifles from the deep shadows at the end of the hall.

One of them was running through the lighted doorway of the Tomlins' room when Gabe stepped back out an instant later. The other was still levering a new round into the chamber, his eyes going round with surprise and terror when he found himself looking down the black bore of Gabe's revolver. Gabe hesitated an instant but the man made the mistake of lifting his rifle. Gabe pulled the trigger and thumbed back the hammer, then saw that he didn't need a second shot. The man's head flew back, and even above the roar of the gunshot Gabe could hear the sharp snap of his neck breaking.

Gabe trotted silently down the hall while the man's body was still crumpling to the floor. Smoke stung his eyes and nose but he was busy remembering the sound of boots that had alerted him, and the already-open door through which one of the assassins had disappeared. Gabe slipped the spare Remington into his right hand and swung into the master bedroom with the knowledge that he'd be facing at least two outlaws inside.

There were three. Two of them were bending over either side of the bed, wrapping a rope around Chester Tomlin's arms. A coal oil lamp burned on a nightstand nearby. The assassin Gabe had already seen in the hall was standing in the shadows across the room with his arm around Jane Tomlin's waist. He had buried the muzzle of a revolver in the fleshy hollow under her chin and now he was grinning in triumph. But Gabe saw that he was so sure of himself he hadn't bothered to cock the revolver.

"Jes' drop them guns," said the outlaw, "or say goodbye to—"

Gabe didn't hesitate. His Remington roared again and the man's lip spurted blood. Two of his teeth shattered while he was still talking, and blood and pieces of his skull splashed across the wall behind him.

The man had assumed Gabe would stop to reconsider. He thought he'd at least have time to finish his sentence. But his life was over before he could even begin to carry out his threat. Jane Tomlin jerked away with a scream as the outlaw's gun arm fell and he stumbled backwards through the open door of an empty closet. Gabe had an instant to wonder about the closet before he turned his attention to the other two men.

Surprise had delayed them. Everything was moving too fast and they wasted a fraction of a second staring at the man falling into the closet. Then they went for their guns but Gabe was already moving toward the outlaw on the nearest side of the bed, a black-haired man with a mean curl to his lip. Gabe smashed the barrel of his right-hand Remington across the man's wrist while he brought his left hand up to eye level. The outlaw's weapon was thudding on the floor when Gabe snapped off a pair of shots at his partner. Two small puffs of dust rose up from the second man's vest and he fell across the bed, pumping blood all over Chester Tomlin's body.

The storekeeper started writhing on the bed, his arms pinned by coils of rope and the weight of the body. He gave Gabe a desperate, pleading look and tried to say something, but a gag stifled his cries. Gabe turned toward the woman, aware that she had stopped screaming. She was looking back at him with vacant eyes.

"Snap out of it," he told her. "It's time to get dressed."

The black-haired man was still bent over and holding his wrist, moaning softly. Gabe ran to the bedroom door and looked out, and heard a soft thud behind him. The black-haired man had dropped to his knees, trying to scoop up his pistol in both hands. Gabe shot him in the neck and began to curse as the man fell on his side, clasping his throat.

"I wanted someone the law could talk to," he muttered bitterly. "Damn it, Mrs. Tomlin, you can't go around in your nightgown. Get some clothes on!"

She was staring at the blood spurting through the outlaw's fingers. Her gaze drifted slowly up toward Gabe, as helpless as a small girl's. "I can't," she said.

Gabe finally noticed the position of her arms, realizing that they were tied behind her back. "Sorry," he said. "How about turning around."

He knew he'd used all five loads in one of the Remingtons. He tucked it behind his belt and slipped the full spare into his shoulder rig. Then he kneeled behind the woman and fumbled with the knots that bound her wrists.

"One of them was waiting in the closet?" he asked as he worked.

Jane Tomlin nodded, her brown curls bobbing around her ears.

"Sure," Gabe murmured. "The other two didn't have time to light a lamp or tie anyone up like this. Will you be all right, Mrs. Tomlin?"

She nodded again, flexing her hands as she felt the rope getting looser. One of her fingers brushed Gabe's palm and a flush warmed his face. He found himself staring at the slope of her back, and the distraction made him a little slow when he heard someone running through the door behind him. Surprise slowed him down even more when he recognized the man from the poker game, Mike Ravis, the player who had vowed revenge after Gabe fooled him with a bluff.

Ravis was rushing him at full speed, holding a pistol high overhead as if he planned to use it like a club. Maybe he was afraid of hitting the woman with a stray bullet, or maybe he wanted Gabe alive long enough to suffer. Wild hatred glittered in his small black eyes as he closed the distance. Gabe was still twisting around on his knees and feeling clumsy.

But long years of habit had already started his hand sweeping under his coat with the first hint of trouble. And as it moved—as he turned to face the killer—he knew he wouldn't have time to pull and cock and aim the revolver before Ravis was on top of him. His fingers closed around the handle of the knife hanging at his side. The blade slipped free as the big pistol began its downward arc above his head.

Gabe ducked beneath the blow and plunged his knife up into the outlaw's belly. The blade slid in smooth just under the ribs and Gabe turned it straight up with a hard thrust. The outlaw's eyes bulged with terror as he felt his heart torn open, then opened wider when Gabe ripped the knife out and jumped back to let the blood flow. The man stared at Gabe for several seconds, his arms hanging helplessly as the hatred returned to his face.

"You son of a bitch," he rasped. "You goddamn dirty son of a bitch."

Then the man's eyes started to fade and Gabe pushed him aside. The body toppled toward the bed, landing across Chester Tomlin's legs. Pools of blood soaked the tumble of sheets and blankets and the storekeeper struggled more fiercely than ever, a touch of hysteria coming into his muffled yells. Gabe watched him without feeling anything, leaning down to wipe the blade on the bedding. He shoved the knife back into its sheath and pulled out the Remington once more, glancing warily toward the door. Then he studied the storekeeper.

"This isn't what you had in mind," said Gabe, "is it?"

Tomlin looked up at him, wide-eyed and straining to say something.

"That's OK," said Gabe. "I'll let the deputies find you just like this. That was the effect you wanted, wasn't it?" He turned toward the woman, trying to make his voice softer. "It's time to leave," he told her. "I know you've had some shocks but you have to hurry up and get some clothes on."

She didn't seem to hear. She was massaging her wrists and

gazing at him with a look he didn't understand at first. "You really aren't working for him, are you," she said. "Could it be that I can really trust you?"

Gabe smiled and said, "That's what I've been trying to tell you, Mrs. Tomlin." He looked around the room. "Otherwise you'd have to believe your husband hired five men just to put on a show." He shook his head in disgust. "I wonder what it cost him."

"It didn't cost him a thing," said Jane Tomlin.

Gabe gave her a surprised look, still watching the doorway from the corner of his eye. The woman had crossed her arms as if to hold herself. She shivered violently, staring at her husband with cold appraising eyes.

"It was my money," she said. "He never had any of his own. He used my money to buy out the store and now he's trying to destroy me with it."

The storekeeper's head thrashed from side to side, his eyes begging her not to believe what she was saying.

"Oh, it's true all right," said the woman. "He wanted everything. But if I have anything to say about it he'll be out in the cold."

Tomlin looked from his wife to Gabe and back again, gradually subsiding beneath the bodies that covered him. A hint of fear came into his expression.

"Come on," Gabe said to the woman. "We really have to go."

"Why?" she asked. "Someone probably heard the shooting and sent for the law already."

"That's what I mean!" Gabe went to the door and glanced down the hall, listening carefully. "What if your husband tries to claim I was part of all this, just to get me out of the way?"

Jane Tomlin frowned.

"That explains why I'm leaving," said Gabe. "You're

leaving with me because that's the only way I can protect you. So dress as fast as you can. I'll be out here.''

Gabe ran to his room to retrieve his warbag, then came back to wait just outside the Tomlin's room. He listened to the rustle of women's clothing as he dug inside the bag, coming up with a loaded cylinder for his revolver.

"As fast as you can," Gabe urged, soft but insistant. "I think I hear someone coming up the street."

He took the Remington from his belt and pulled out the spent cylinder, replacing it with the spare that was already packed with powder and balls and charged with caps. Steps sounded on the front porch as he put the Remington back in his belt.

"I'm coming in to get you," said Gabe.

But Jane Tomlin appeared in the doorway, wearing a faded blue dress and carrying the same yellow carpetbag her husband had used to bring the ransom. She jumped when knuckles pounded on the front door. Gabe put a finger to his lips and led her toward the rear of the house. Someone smashed the door down and pounded up the front stairs just as Gabe and the woman started down the back stairs toward the kitchen.

At the back door Gabe held his breath and lifted his Remington to shoulder level before he went out. The dark yard seemed deserted. He signaled the woman to follow him across the yard and through a gate in the high back fence. A dog barked as they went by a carriage house and emerged onto another street. Gabe winced when he heard the dog.

"We have to keep moving," he said. "Are you still all right, Mrs. Tomlin?"

"I think you can start calling me Jane," she said with a laugh. "After everything we've been through together."

Gabe laughed too, then gave the woman a look of respect.

"I don't have to worry about you, do I? You're a woman who can take it."

Jane held her head a little higher, her eyes flashing with a hard kind of pride. "I never used to think so," she said. "But maybe you're right."

But then they crossed the main street just a block away from the jail and a sad, wistful look replaced the triumph. Gabe glanced at the dark stone building, wondering what had caused the change.

"By the way," said Jane, "where are we going?"

"Sam McClure's house."

"The marshal?"

Gabe nodded. "I think we need a friend."

CHAPTER TEN

Gabe sat alone by a small fire, deep inside the same pine grove he had spent so many hours watching a few days before. Dawn was showing itself as specks of silver through the branches when Gabe heard the beat of a single horse coming along the Black Hills road. It turned off toward the grove, its sound muffled in the deep grass.

Marshal Sam McClure appeared in the ring of firelight a minute later, leading the horse behind him. He tied it beside Gabe's pony and approached the fire with an accusing look.

"I hope you're ready to do some talking," he said. "That was a hell of a mess you left behind. Thorne's given orders to have you arrested."

"Sit down," said Gabe. "We'll have a smoke."

He reached for a small medicine pipe lying on a bed of pine needles at his side. The bowl and the short stem, carved from soapstone, glowed a dusky red in the light from the fire. Gabe poked two fingers into a pouch hanging from his belt and transferred a wad of tobacco to the pipe.

McClure frowned at the procedure and said, "What's this all about?"

"Go ahead and sit," Gabe urged. "This will be our council fire. Breathing the same smoke will bring our minds into harmony."

"I don't *need* any harmony, damn it. I need answers. What happened tonight?"

Gabe ignored him, calmly lifting a coal from the fire with a pair of sticks. He used the coal to light the tobacco, sucking the smoke deep into his lungs. Then he held the pipe up to the marshal.

"Go ahead," he said. "You'll feel better. Then we can talk and I know my words will be heard with clarity."

McClure rolled his eyes, then dropped to the ground beside Gabe and put the stem to his mouth. The embers in the bowl glowed red before he handed the pipe back to Gabe.

"You should feel honored to smoke this pipe," said Gabe. "I received it from a great Oglala chief before he was hanged at Fort Laramie."

"What did he do?"

"You mean his crime?" Gabe said with a bitter smile. "He rescued a white woman from the Cheyenne and brought her in. But they figured he was just another redskin . . ."

"Yeah I know," McClure growled. "The Army did some pretty stupid things."

A harsh light flared in Gabe's eyes for a moment, then died away. "That's history," he said. "Did you find a safe place for Mrs. Tomlin?"

"One of my deputies took her home to stay with his wife." Gabe started to say something but the marshal cut him off. "I trust the man. He'll keep his mouth shut no matter what happens."

"And keep her out of sight?"

"She won't even go near a window for a couple days."

McClure studied Gabe's face across the flames. "You really believe that Tomlin's trying to have her killed?"

Gabe shrugged. "There's only three choices. One is Tomlin. Number two is Frank Haywood, and I don't think you like that idea."

McClure shook his head. "I know him too well."

"All right, then. Choice number three would be someone else we haven't even thought of."

"Just for the money, in other words. With everything else thrown in to make us look in the wrong direction." McClure stared into the fire. "Seems like a lot of trouble."

"Not to mention the problem that Tomlin brought up himself: how would anyone else know about the property Haywood wanted?"

The marshal frowned at that. "It does keep pointing back to Tomlin, doesn't it."

"And he works overtime to point the other way. Remember the day they brought Haywood in? Remember Tomlin saying he'd seen the rancher having a talk with the man who took his wife?"

McClure nodded and said, "I was thinkin' the same thing. The body came in under a blanket and went straight to the undertaker. Tomlin never had a chance to see what the man looked like."

Gabe nodded and said, "There's something else. Those men in the house tonight had an ambush all set up for me."

"But everyone in town saw you guarding Mrs. Tomlin. It wasn't any secret."

"That's not the point. *They knew what room I was in.* Two of them were waiting at the end of the hall, watching my door. They meant to kill me as soon as I came out."

McClure gave Gabe a doubtful look. "You're still alive. Did you just get lucky or what?"

"I expected them, that's all. I went on the assumption that

Tomlin wanted me dead, too. So when no one tried to get into my room"—Gabe shrugged—"then I figured they had to be in the hall."

"That's a lot of figurin', son. Was this all going on while you were running to the door?"

Gabe shook his head. "I didn't want to have to do any thinking at all by then. It's faster if I've already thought out the different ways it could happen, and what I should do."

McClure nodded slowly, giving Gabe a closer look. "That's pretty sharp," he said. "You're not just a fast man with a gun, are you?"

Gabe shrugged. "I had a lot of time to kill."

"Uh-huh," said McClure.

The marshal kept looking at Gabe, trying to take his measure, but the scrutiny was uncomfortable for a man who'd been raised among the Oglalas. Even after many years among the whites, Gabe still tended to look down or off to one side during conversations. He considered it a sign of respect. A direct stare, on the other hand, seemed aggressive or hostile. When such a stare began to make him angry, Gabe would force himself to remember that meeting someone's eyes is how the whites *show* respect.

"So," he said, "can you arrest Tomlin and get Mr. Haywood out of jail?"

A dark mood settled over the marshal. "I'm not sure, Gabe. Just because we *know* something, you and I, doesn't mean I can prove it."

"But what about the claims he made? What about the killers knowing which room I was in?"

McClure shook his head. "He can just say he made a mistake about seeing Frank with that first man you killed. He can say he believed Frank was guilty, and wanted to make sure he was convicted. People would understand. And if you get accused of being part of it, then it'll just be your word against his on who shot at you where.''

"But you saw the house tonight. You saw the bullet holes in my door and the man at the end of the hall."

McClure shrugged. "Could've happened anytime. It don't mean too much where a man falls. On the other hand there was also another note."

Gabe's shoulders sagged a little. "I suppose it was like the first one," he said. "Setting conditions for Mrs. Tomlin's release."

"Remember the guy you knifed?"

Gabe's lips twisted in a scornful look.

"The note was in his pocket. It said Tomlin could have his wife back if he didn't testify against Frank Haywood."

"Damn it," said Gabe, "I should have looked for something like that."

"Don't be too hard on yourself, son. I bet you didn't have a lot of time to fool around once the fur started to fly."

"It's still gonna make things worse."

"I have to admit," said McClure, "Tomlin's been pretty clever. He's made everything look one way and it'll be hard to prove any different."

"You can find the same public records I did. That'll show how much he needed to control his wife's money."

"Sure. I'll do it today. But he can show that he hired you to *protect* her life."

"That only shows he was trying to cover up. Trying to stay out of jail."

"That's how it looks to you and me, maybe. There'll even be some other folks in town who have their doubts. But we have to *prove* it in court."

"I'm beginning to understand the attractions of a lynch mob," said Gabe. "That little runt of a bastard better get what's coming to him or I'll take care of it myself."

"Then I'd maybe have to arrest you," said McClure. "As much as I'd hate to do it." He sighed and looked off through the trees. "Things are changing out here. You know that. We have to follow the law."

"Or keep from getting caught, anyway."

McClure squinted at Gabe. "Tomlin's pretty good at that himself—at using the law to get what he wants. Maybe that'd put you and him in the same class."

"Bullshit! It comes down to whether you're right or wrong."

"I don't think Judge Wilcox would see it that way. And I'll tell you something else, he's no friend of mine. Or Frank's. Whatever proof we come up with will have to be damn good."

"What about the man hiding in the closet? How did he get in there?"

"That ain't much of a point. People have been known to climb through windows."

Gabe scowled. "What if Tomlin was seen talking to one of the men I killed? They were all strangers, weren't they?"

"I'm sure that's what we'll find out. I've already told my deputies to ask around town. But don't hold your breath, my friend. Half the strangers who come into town will stop at his store for supplies. He could arrange things right there and nobody'd ever be the wiser."

"Christ!" said Gabe. "There's still his finances, right? His bank records and stock deals and so on."

"That'll be part of the picture, maybe. It won't mean much by itself."

"It'll show why he wanted his wife out of the way, won't it? Especially if she testifies she was getting ready to leave him."

McClure gave him a sharp look. "Did she tell you that?"

"It was just a guess. But she didn't deny it."

"The thing is, Gabe, she *wasn't* killed. All a judge'n jury will see are two abduction attempts. It'll look like he did everything he could to *take care* of Jane. Hell, he put up a valuable piece of land and ten thousand dollars just to get her back. And he hired you."

"No he didn't," Gabe snapped.

"You know what I mean, son. I'm talking about appearances."

"Something Chester Tomlin is good at."

"You have to give the man his due."

"I don't have to do a damn thing."

Gabe was too busy frowning into the fire to see the glint of amusement in the old marshal's eyes.

"I know it's hard," McClure said gently. "Tomlin kind of roped you in, didn't he? I bet there ain't been too many people who could do that."

"It's been a while, I guess."

McClure chuckled. "Then you're a better man than most of us, son. But you're still just a man. It pisses you off, bein' used like that."

"He won't get away with it."

McClure studied Gabe while the fire crackled between them. He looked into the hard grey eyes and then he sighed. "No, I guess not," he said. "Maybe there's something to this smoke business, because we got harmony when it comes to that."

Gabe offered the marshal a grim smile, but his expression remained thoughtful. "There's one question I wish I knew the answer to," he said. "Maybe it'd be the key to everything else."

McClure tilted his head to one side, content to wait while Gabe put his thoughts in order.

"Everything makes sense," said Gabe. "All the way back to staging that first abduction. Who knows, maybe Mrs.

Tomlin wasn't supposed to come back alive the first time. But at least he made it look like there was a threat. So the son of a bitch asks me to help. Then he pays five more men to kill me and stage another abduction—''

"Don't forget that it didn't work, by the way. You oughta be proud. If it weren't for you, Mrs. Tomlin probably *would* be dead by now.''

"That's what I mean. Those men would carry her off and then they'd find her body somewhere. Everybody'd say, 'poor Chester Tomlin.' Then they'd hang Frank Haywood and feel good about it, leaving poor Chester Tomlin with all his wife's money and half the real estate in Sidney.''

McClure was nodding. "Sounds about right,'' he said.

"Except for my question. Why Frank Haywood? Do you know of any problems those two ever had before last week?''

McClure's eyelids fluttered. "Problems?'' he said.

"There had to be something, marshal. Tomlin went after that quarter section of land like he knew what he was doing. He forced the owner to sell it to him. Then he used it against Haywood.''

McClure frowned and looked away. "I see your point,'' he said.

"So I'm wondering why Tomlin picked on Haywood in the first place. Out of all the people in Sidney.''

"Wish I could say, son.'' The sun had come up and now it was filtering into the grove, the golden light shifting across the marshal's face. "But I'll look into it, that's for sure. Where will you be?''

"Right here, at least for the day. Seems like a good time to catch up on some sleep.''

"And tonight?''

Gabe shrugged, then winked at the marshal.

"Don't forget what I said about the sheriff,'' McClure warned.

"I expected it." Suddenly Gabe sat a little straighter. "That's another idea," he said. "I know Thorne and Haywood didn't get along, but the sheriff sure seems ready to jump when Tomlin tells him to. Kind of makes you wonder about *his* finances, doesn't it?"

McClure was looking at Gabe. "You ever think about a career in law enforcement, son?"

Gabe laughed.

"Uh-huh," said the marshal, "that's what I was afraid of. But maybe you'll change your mind someday."

"I'm sorry I laughed, marshal. There oughta be more men like you wearing stars. But my stick just doesn't float that way."

"Yeah, well." McClure got to his feet and stood by the fire a moment, wearing the familiar expression of mild amusement. "You be careful in town. Thorne may be mean but he ain't stupid."

Gabe nodded and watched the marshal walk over to untie his horse. "How do I find you?" he asked. "In case I get any more ideas."

"Or get into more trouble," McClure said drily. "I'm in one of Tomlin's hotels, the St. Pierre. Room three-seventeen. You can come up the back stairs." He climbed into the saddle. "What about if I need to talk to you again?" he said. "Do I gotta come all the way out here?"

Gabe laughed again and said, "I hope not. Just leave word with Sarah."

McClure grinned back at him. "Lordy, I sure wish envy weren't a sin," he said with a sigh. "I'll never get to heaven now."

CHAPTER ELEVEN

Sam McClure's last words came back to Gabe later that night as he worked his way through the dark streets of Sidney. He went through them one at a time, slipping into the thickest shadow he could find and waiting until his eyes got used to the darkness. The waiting came easy because he believed it necessary, but it was also a good time to think and to remember things like Sam McClure's talk of heaven, which made Gabe smile.

He also used the time to listen for any sounds, to watch for any reflected light or subtle shift in the shadows around him—in other words, anything that might betray the presence of another man. When he was sure the street or alley was empty he moved one street closer to the saloon with the shanties out back.

Gabe was a little surprised that he didn't come across any sheriff's deputies. If Thorne was still looking for him it would have made sense to post at least one man near Sarah Prater's crib. The thing between them was no secret. Gabe wondered if the sheriff had already tried and given up on the idea. Maybe he didn't have enough men for the job, or maybe something had happened during the day to change his mind. Gabe was happy to reach the back of the saloon without being detected, but it also made him uneasy. He would have felt better if he knew why.

He hesitated in front of her door, glancing up at the high window under the eaves. It glowed faintly with the dull yellow light from a coal oil lamp, but Gabe had no way of knowing whether Sarah was alone. He hadn't seen her in two days, since coming by to tell her about staying with the Tomlins. He'd also told her he didn't know how long it would last, and he didn't think it was right for her to waste a lot of time waiting for him. Now it seemed just as unfair to bust in on her.

Then Gabe thought some more about the tall redhead with the lively brown eyes, and the way those eyes had glowed when she was looking at him. He hoped he wasn't about to make a fool of himself, but an instinct told him to take a chance on her. He knocked once, very lightly, then opened the door and slipped inside.

Sarah was sitting on the bed and reading a newspaper, her back propped against the wall. She wore a very long robe of red silk that still didn't cover the length of her legs. She looked up from the paper without surprise, a slow smile parting her lips. "Well, well," she said. "I was beginning to think you really did run off with the Tomlin woman."

"Is that what you're reading?" said Gabe.

Sarah shook her head. "It happened too late for the paper. But it's almost the only thing people have been talking about."

"What do they say?"

"It's more what Chester Tomlin says. You were working with Frank Haywood all the time and now you're holding the woman against her will. You're trying to make Tomlin change his testimony so the sheriff will let Frank go.''

"And those five dead men in his house? How does he explain them?''

"Getting rid of accomplices who might talk, I guess.'' Sarah shrugged. "It's not like the sheriff is asking too many questions. Tomlin's also saying you might've run off with his wife because you fell in love with her.'' Sarah grinned at Gabe. "Or her money, anyway. I was beginning to think that's where you were tonight, getting cozy with Jane.''

"*Plain* Jane,'' said Gabe. "She's too worn down to turn a man's head. And she's married.''

"You didn't look close enough or you'd have seen that the one thing is only because of the other. Make her happy and you'd be surprised how pretty she could be.''

Gabe looked surprised and Sarah laughed.

"Women notice a lot of things men never see,'' she said. "Especially about other women. Jane Tomlin's got plenty of life in her—plenty of what it takes to please a man.''

Gabe grinned and said, "Maybe I did notice a little of that.''

"I just bet you did.''

"But you'll be happy to know I've been sleeping alone all day, hiding out from the sheriff.''

"Good thing,'' said Sarah. "Your midnight massacre caused a lot of excitement around here. Thorne and his men were riding in and out of town all day.''

"He didn't look in the right places.''

"What about Jane? Have you got her waiting outside?''

Gabe laughed and said, "Sure, I've always wanted to have two women at the same time. I figured you wouldn't mind.''

Sarah dropped the paper on the floor and stretched herself with a slow, tantalizing grace. The way a cat stretches. Her robe fell open along the length of her legs. "If this isn't enough for you," she said, "then you can go to hell."

Gabe shrugged, still grinning. "So I was wrong," he said.

"I'm glad I wasn't wrong about *you*. I knew you'd show up." She patted the bed beside her. "Come over and tell me the whole thing, lover. Where's the Tomlin woman staying?"

"One of the marshal's deputies is guarding her."

"Anyone I know?" Sarah said archly.

"McClure didn't mention the name. But he trusts the man to keep Tomlin away from her."

Sarah frowned and said, "Keep her away from her *husband?*"

Gabe realized how much had happened since the last time they talked. He sat down and started to tell the story while Sarah listened with avid interest. Tomlin's business acquisitions were one of the biggest surprises, and one of them seemed to worry her. "Are you sure he owns the *bank?*" she said.

"Controlling interest, anyway. About eighty percent. Why?"

But Sarah just shook her head and asked more questions about the battle in Tomlin's house. She wanted to know every detail, as if she was trying to see it in her head. Then she asked what it was that made the Tomlin woman think her husband was trying to kill her. Gabe explained his guess about her getting ready to leave him, and Sarah laughed with delight.

"What's so funny?" said Gabe.

"Poor Chester," said Sarah. "I think it's wonderful! Maybe our plain Jane has found someone else after all."

Gabe nodded, accepting the possibility and liking it better the more he thought about it. One reason he liked it, he admitted to himself, was that it would make things simpler for him in the long run. He didn't want her giving him any looks when she found herself alone.

"So the whole thing has been a phony?" said Sarah. "Acted out like some kind of play?"

"So far."

"You really think that funny little man could be so clever?"

"That's the best part, as far as he was concerned. He's such a coward and he looks like such a fool that no one would have thought about it. It still won't be easy to prove what happened."

"He won't get away with it, will he?"

"I hope not. But there's still one question no one can answer for me, something that keeps the whole picture from falling into place."

"And the question is . . ."

"Why Frank Haywood? Of all the people around here, why did Tomlin—"

Sarah laughed and said, "That's easy! It also answers your question about Jane leaving her husband."

"Of course!" said Gabe, giving Sarah a look of wonder. "Christ, how blind can one man be? She kept staring at the jail every time we went by, with the longest face I ever saw. Kept making a point of saying she didn't know the man personally—"

"Maybe you didn't *want* to see it." Sarah lowered her head to give him a wise, half-amused look from under her long lashes. "Maybe you didn't want to believe she was in love with someone else."

"But I'm glad she is. I've never stayed in one place long enough to—"

Sarah was shaking her head. "Doesn't matter, Gabe. Every man wants a woman to want him."

He stopped talking long enough to look at the woman

stretched out on the bed at his side. He saw the sharp intelligence that made her eyes sparkle, the soft red curl of her hair, the full lips and the wide downturned mouth. "I'm hoping that's what I have you for," he said.

Her expression didn't change for a moment. She kept looking at him with a half-smile that could have meant anything. Then her nostrils flared and Gabe saw her breasts swelling higher and higher beneath the scarlet robe. Something else began to swell, pressing up against his trousers. He squirmed and Sarah looked down at the source of his discomfort.

"Stand up," she said.

Gabe did as he was told and Sarah turned herself until she was sitting on the edge of the bed in front of him. The robe fell away from her breasts but she was busy staring at the long bulge of his shaft. She covered part of it with her hand and began to stroke it, closing her eyes. Her lips parted and Gabe could hear her breathing.

"Take off your pants," she whispered.

The buttons were hard to work with so much pressure on them, but suddenly his shaft sprang free and Sarah took it between her hands while he struggled to free his legs from the trousers. Then she closed her eyes again and pressed her cheek against him.

"I've been thinking about this for two days," she murmured.

Her tongue curled out to taste him, curled around his shaft and moved up slowly until she opened her mouth to engulf him in sudden hunger. Still he felt her tongue, swirling around and around as she pulled him into her mouth. She clung to him and groaned with satisfaction.

Sarah put her arms around him and turned him toward the bed, twisting and turning with him until he was lying on his back and she was kneeling between his legs. For a while he watched her head moving over him, thinking that he wanted to remove his shirt and shoulder holster. Then he closed his eyes to concentrate on the pleasure she was giving him. At first he could feel her tongue separate from her lips, and separate from the long fingers that followed them up and down. Then it all blended into one fiery sensation that threatened to explode and burn itself out.

Sarah knew. She lifted her head and winked at him and said, "Not yet, lover."

She was still holding him in both hands and now she straddled him, throwing her head back while she lowered herself onto his shaft. She shuddered and her breasts began to quiver. Gabe filled his hands with them as Sarah's hips moved in slow circles. The red silk robe swirled around her body. Gabe leaned up to bury his face between the swaying breasts and Sarah hugged him to her, moving faster and then faster still.

Gabe felt her muscles going tight and knew he didn't have to hold himself back, didn't have to wait. A helpless urgency came into her breathing and then she gasped, pulling away to look down at him with wide, startled eyes. She cried out and he drove himself up into her, grinning fiercely as his body flooded with ecstasy. They held onto each other for a while and then their bodies began to melt together. Sarah leaned down to unbutton Gabe's shirt, first, her breasts hanging cradled between her arms. Then she lay on top of him, pressing them against his chest. Suddenly she giggled.

"I guess I was ready," she said. "Is that what it's like for a man?"

Gabe nodded, brushing his face against the softness of her hair.

"How do you *stand* it?" said Sarah. "How do you make yourself wait?"

"It's only what a woman like you deserves."

Sarah giggled again, a soft sound coming out of her throat. Her breath felt hot against Gabe's ear. "Well, now I know how much to appreciate it," she said.

"It's also selfish, you know. I have to admit it. It's like waiting till you're good and hungry before you eat."

"Eat what, lover?"

Gabe laughed and said, "Whatever you're hungry for. And no offense, but right now that means steak."

Sarah sat up to look at him. "You're not going out, are you?"

Gabe shook his head. "Not if the sheriff is still looking for me."

"That's what worried me. Because I haven't heard different."

"I didn't think so. But it seemed strange that there wasn't someone watching your place."

"Not so strange when you know the reason." Sarah let Gabe slip out of her and lay down beside him, her eyes dancing with a look of mischief. "Chester Tomlin came by this morning. He offered me seven thousand dollars to pump you for information."

"I'll be damned!" said Gabe. "He wanted you to find out where his wife is, right?"

She nodded while Gabe studied her with a troubled frown.

"Is that why you kept asking about her," he said. "Were you planning to sell me out?"

Sarah laughed and said, "Only if you deserved it." But Gabe kept frowning and Sarah's eyes flashed with anger. "Don't worry," she said, "I'm not about to help that bastard kill his wife."

"Well, no," said Gabe. "I know that. I mean, now that you know what he has in mind . . ."

"Listen to me, lover. I was *never* planning to sell you out."

Gabe was still thinking of the questions she'd asked but he saw the stormy look in her eyes and decided to let it go. "Sorry," he said. "I should've known better."

"The hell with that," said Sarah. "You'd be crazy *not* to worry. Seven thousand dollars is a lot of money."

Gabe grinned. "Was it hard to turn down?"

"Who said anything about turning it down? Why would I turn down seven thousand dollars?" Sarah watched the confusion growing in Gabe's eyes, then gave him a playful wink. "So now the question is: what do you want me to say?"

Gabe understood immediately, and felt an even deeper appreciation for the woman beside him. "You mean you're willing to help?" he asked. "You'd tell him—"

"Whatever you tell me to tell him." Sarah grinned. "Otherwise I don't get the other part of the money." Then she laughed. "I just have to get the down payment out of his bank before he finds out I lied!"

"It's exactly what we need," Gabe told Sam McClure an hour later. "It would make a perfect trap."

The marshal sat up straighter in his bed, rubbing a hand over his eyes. "And you're sure she wants to do it?"

"Tomlin only gave her two thousand dollars to start with," said Gabe. "She gets *five* thousand if she delivers."

"It might be risky for her."

"Maybe. But you could arrest the bastard as soon as he makes his move."

"He might not join the party."

"He probably won't," said Gabe. "Not that coward. But you'd still have enough evidence to arrest him, wouldn't you? If we pick a place and it gets attacked, and he's the only one Sarah talked to about that particular place . . ."

McClure closed his eyes and for a moment it looked as if he was sleeping again. It was hard to tell in the darkened room. Gabe and the marshal had decided against lighting a lantern when Gabe first came in, in case one of the sheriff's men was watching McClure's hotel.

"OK," McClure finally said. "Sure. That would be good enough to satisfy a judge. But what if we need Sarah's testimony to convict."

"Look at it this way: she doesn't want him where he can get at her."

The marshal nodded. "It'd be even better if we could keep one of the attackers alive. Get him to tell who hired him."

"We'll do it."

McClure peered at Gabe in the darkness. "You weren't so lucky last night."

"None of the fools wanted to quit, damn it! That's not my fault. But if they see the odds are all against 'em . . ."

McClure scratched the side of his neck. "That could be tricky, though. Tomlin might suspect something if I pull all my deputies off the street."

"Could you get 'em from opposite shifts? It shouldn't take more than a couple days."

"Less than that," said McClure. "Thorne sent a wire to Judge Wilcox. So now they've set Frank's trial date for the day after tomorrow, as soon as the judge gets back.

"They're rushing this right along, aren't they?"

"I think they're getting nervous, Gabe. Thanks to you. Things keep going wrong, so they hope to convict Frank before the whole thing unravels."

"Then Tomlin will make his move tomorrow night. That's even easier. All we need to do is figure out where."

"That's *all?*" said McClure. "This is my town, you know. I don't like the idea of starting a war here."

"Then do it out on the prairie. What about Haywood's line shack?"

The marshal was shaking his head. "I couldn't make any arrests out there. It's not my jurisdiction."

"Don't you ever get tired of all these rules, McClure?"

"Hell yes! But I ain't gonna give Wilcox any excuse to mess us up."

"All right, all right. Then all we need is a house where no one's living. Maybe in a neighborhood where there aren't too many people—"

Gabe was stopped by the sound of a gunshot echoing through the quiet streets. A second later he heard a shrill whistle.

"Shit!" said McClure. He threw off his covers and jumped for a pair of trousers and a coat folded over a chair. "Something's happening at the jail. That's the signal for trouble."

Gabe ran for the door with McClure a few steps behind him, still strapping on his gunbelt.

"Where the hell do you think you're going?" said the marshal. "What if this is a trap for *you?*"

Gabe looked at McClure as they ran down the stairs. "Have to take the chance, I guess."

"There is a solution" said the older man. "Thorne would have a harder time arresting one of my deputies."

Gabe laughed. "This is a trap, all right," he said. "But I think it's your trap and I'm the one who's caught."

CHAPTER TWELVE

McClure fished a tin star out of his pocket and passed it to Gabe, who pinned it to his shirt as they ran through the hotel lobby. A clock over the registration desk told them it was already after one o'clock. Outside, they saw one of McClure's men running down the street and joined him in the race toward the jail. A second deputy was already waiting near the steel-plated door, along with the lookout who had fired the shot and sounded the whistle. He was a blond-haired man with freckled skin and a missing tooth.

"Not sure what happened," he told the marshal with a worried look. "There was sort of a groan and kind of a rustling sound."

McClure frowned at him and then cocked his head to listen for any further noises from the basement cells, trying to guess what they might have meant. But two minutes had passed since the alarm and McClure didn't want any more time to go by. Gabe could see the decision in his eyes and was already reaching under his coat when the marshal pulled his own revolver.

"We're going in," said McClure.

He tried the door while the other four men bunched around him with their weapons drawn. Then he pounded his fists against the steel plates. "You've got ten seconds to open this fucking door!" he yelled. "One, two—"

"You got no rights in here," a voice yelled back, sounding muffled through the heavy door. "This building is county property."

"Better get behind a desk, Thorne. Three, four, five—"

"What the hell are you talking about?"

"Three sticks of dynamite and a fifteen-second fuse. Six, seven—"

"Now hold on a minute."

"I light the fuse when I'm done counting, Thorne. Eight—"

"I said *wait,* goddamn it!"

The men behind McClure grinned at each other when they heard the sound of heavy bolts being thrown back. The door opened a crack and McClure pushed it wide. Thorne and a young bearded deputy with sharp black eyes were waiting with their guns in their hands, but they backed away from the small army bearing down on them.

"You'll lose your job over this," the sheriff told McClure. "You can't come bustin' in and—"

"Shut up!" said McClure. "I want to talk to your prisoner, *now.*"

"You can't—"

"Get the keys, Gabe."

The other three marshals crowded around the sheriff and the young deputy, taking away their guns while Gabe went through the gate toward the desks.

"You no-account half-breed bastard," Thorne yelled after

him. "I'll see you in jail on five counts of murder. Maybe six."

Gabe acted as if he didn't hear anything. He was pulling drawers out of the desks and letting them fall to the floor, scattering the contents. There was a heavy ring of keys in the fourth drawer he opened. He picked them out of a jumbled pile on the floor and the sheriff's fury blazed even hotter.

"And *you*," he roared, glaring at McClure, "you're aiding and abetting a fugitive. You'll lose your job and go to jail."

McClure dismissed the bull-necked sheriff with one scornful look while he bolted the front entrance again to keep anyone from interfering. Gabe was already unlocking the door leading to the cells. He swung the door back and the town lawmen herded the county lawmen down the stairs.

There was only one weak-burning coal oil lamp at the bottom of the landing, its yellow light evaporating in the blackness just a few feet out. Gabe took the lamp down from its hook and led the party through a narrow passage between a stone wall on one side and thick iron bars on the other. Everything was covered with heavy drops of condensation and the air itself seemed full of water. Gabe had to fight back a choking sensation and an urge to run back up the stairs. He wondered if he would be able to survive imprisonment in these cells.

The passage turned and the first thing Gabe saw around the corner was a soft glare of white high up on one of the bars at the far end. He shouted and broke into a run, holding the lantern up ahead of him. A cold dread touched his heart when the light fell on a dark form hanging from a bedsheet inside the cell. Then Gabe saw two big hands gripping the bars. They fell away while he was still running toward them.

"My God!" he heard Thorne say. "The son of a bitch hung himself!"

"I'm sure you're real surprised," said McClure.

Gabe handed the lantern to one of the other deputies and started fumbling with the keys in front of the cell door. The sheriff pushed through and took them out of his hand.

"Here," he said, "it's this one."

Thorne opened the door and McClure was the first to rush in, grabbing his friend's body around the legs. He looked like a boy trying to lift his father except for the grim determination burning in his eyes. McClure heaved up and the rancher's head flopped to one side. Gabe also took a grip and helped to hold the big man against the bars, not sure whether he was still breathing. The freckle-faced deputy was working on the knot in the bedsheet but the rancher's weight had pulled it tight. Gabe held onto Haywood with one arm while he took the knife from under his coat and sliced through the sheet. Then he helped McClure ease the rancher's body to the floor.

The marshal dropped to his knees and held his ear over his friend's mouth while the other men gathered around them in a silent, somber circle. After a few seconds McClure looked up at Thorne and said, "I'll kill you for this."

"Now wait a minute," said the sheriff. "We was upstairs. You saw us. We had no way o' knowin'—"

Haywood's body lurched up and he coughed with a terrible strangling sound, his eyes snapping open with a white look of panic. He clawed at the sheet that was still tied tight around his throat, coughing again in spasms and banging the back of his head on the stone floor. McClure grabbed Haywood's head and cradled it in his arms while Gabe struggled with the sheet.

The rancher quickly realized he could breathe and stopped thrashing around, making it easier for Gabe to untie the knot. The air passing through his throat made a painful rasping sound. Then Haywood recognized who was working over him and his expression hardened into anger. Gabe ignored it, picking at the knot and glancing up in time to see a furtive, worried look in the sheriff's eyes. Gabe wondered if McClure had noticed.

But the marshal was intent on something else. He was probing the rancher's scalp with his fingers, frowning as he concentrated on an area just behind the right ear. Haywood winced and pulled his head away. McClure looked up at the sheriff and then his deputy, one at a time. The deputy looked down.

"So he tried to kill himself?" said McClure.

"I don't know," Thorne insisted. "We was upstairs—"

"Don't tell me that!" McClure jumped to his feet and stood in front of the sheriff, his body trembling violently. He looked like a man about to lose control and Thorne shrank back from him, but the marshal's voice came out low and deadly. "I suppose the first thing Frank tried to do was hit himself over the head, is that it?" McClure leaned forward and Thorne leaned back a little further. "And then when he found out he couldn't kill himself that way he just naturally put a sheet around his neck and tried to strangle himself. Is that your story, Thorne?"

"How the hell should I know?"

McClure turned on the young deputy with the coal black beard and sharp black eyes. "What about you, Steve? You think Frank tried to kill himself?"

The deputy glanced at Thorne and said, "Well . . ."

"He don't know nothin' either," said the sheriff. "We was both—"

"Oh I *forgot*," said McClure. "You were upstairs. So *you* don't know how he got that bump on his scalp."

"He probably done it just now. Hittin' it on the floor."

"On the *side,* behind the ear?"

Gabe saw Haywood weakly shaking his head. The rancher

was lying on the floor and massaging his throat while he glared up at Thorne with a look that Gabe remembered from their first meeting. It was the same way he'd looked at Chester Tomlin.

"I don't know how he done it," said Thorne. "I don't give a shit, either. He's the crazy bastard that tried to kill himself."

McClure's hand slapped the side of Thorne's face and a veil dropped over the sheriff's eyes.

"Easy to do that when you got the drop on someone," said Thorne. "But we'll even things out one o' these days."

"Count on it," McClure said. "I sure ain't afraid of a coward who'd try to kill a man in his own jail cell."

"Me!" said Thorne. "*I* was the one who showed you which key to use. I helped you get into the cell."

"Sure, after you did everything you could to delay us upstairs. You'd probably just come upstairs yourself."

"Try to prove it, little man."

"You're forgetting Frank's still alive. *He's* the one who's gonna hang you by your fat neck."

The bearded deputy threw a worried sideways look at his boss.

"It's his word against mine and you know it," said Thorne. "A convicted felon against the sheriff of Cheyenne County."

"You're wrong so many ways I don't know where to start, Thorne. Frank ain't been convicted yet, for one thing. But your biggest mistake was throwing in with the wrong side."

The deputy's sharp black eyes were still troubled with doubt. There was also a hint of doubt in the sheriff's expression, which he couldn't quite mask. McClure jumped on what he saw.

"Enjoy yourself tomorrow," he sneered at Thorne. "After Wilcox hears the evidence Friday it's gonna be you and Tomlin down here, waiting for a rope.''

"We'll see whose neck gets snapped, you bastard."

But McClure had made his point. He turned his back on the sheriff to squat beside Haywood again. "Can you stand?" he said.

Haywood nodded thickly and sat up, rolling onto his knees before he lumbered to his feet. McClure and Gabe each held one arm, leading the big man out into the passage with the marshal's deputies close behind.

"Hey," said Thorne. "Where are you going with my prisoner?"

McClure laughed with real amusement, looking back at the sheriff and shaking his head. "You got balls of brass, Harry. I have to give you that. You try to kill a man and then you demand him back so you can try again." He looked at his men and said, "Tell you what, let's leave the sheriff and his deputy down here for a while—"

"Hey!"

"Go ahead, lock the door. They might as well get used to it."

The blond deputy grinned, showing his missing tooth as he slammed the cell door and turned the key in the lock. Thorne grabbed the bars and shook the door.

"You can't take my prisoner!" he yelled after the marshal. "Bring him back here."

"Don't worry, Harry," McClure called back, still moving along the passage. "Just call it protective custody. He'll be there for the trial."

"Come back here, you son of a bitch!"

"Relax, Harry. We'll leave the keys in your office." McClure was still chuckling. "They'll hear you cryin' clear to Lincoln. Someone's bound to come a'running."

They went up the stairs, moving slowly behind the rancher. His breath whistled in his throat and behind them the sheriff was still rattling the door of his cell, yelling at McClure. The marshal scowled and shook his head. "Some day," he said softly. "Some day we're *really* gonna tangle."

They went through the office and out onto the boardwalk, crossing to a darker side street that led them away from the jail. Thorne's calls for help faded and died, leaving only the silence of the sleeping town. Gabe made a noise sucking the cool night air into his lungs, and McClure gave him an appreciative glance.

"It does taste sweet," the marshal said with a sigh. "That was always my favorite part of night duty, not breathing the dust that gets stirred up during the day. How're you doing, Frank?"

Haywood nodded, then tried for his first words. "Goddamn glad to be breathing," he said with a grin. His voice was rough but there was no mistake about the depth of his feeling.

"What happened down there?"

"I only know parts of it." Haywood cleared his throat, winced, then kept going. "I was asleep, I guess. My head near the bars. They must've hit me a pretty good lick, 'cause I don't remember that sheet goin' 'round my neck."

McClure scowled. "I wish you'd seen who did it."

"Shit," said Haywood, "don't matter whether it was Thorne himself or his deputy. All I know is I can't breathe all of a sudden, and *that* sure woke me up. I also heard a gunshot, didn't I? And a whistle?"

"I had a man outside the jail," said the marshal. "Twenty-four hours a day. I wanted to tell you about it but Thorne wouldn't let anyone in to see you."

"I don't care! I'd still be hangin' from the bars if it weren't for you."

"You can thank Mr. Conrad, actually. He gave me the idea."

The rancher squinted at Gabe, the good humor going out of his eyes. "I don't get it."

"You will," McClure told him. "The thing is, we got to you in time."

"Just barely. I tried to grab the bars after I come out of it but I couldn't get the right grip—couldn't even get enough air to yell. Not that it would've done any good. But then I heard you upstairs and I hung on as long as I could." He shuddered with the memory of how close it had been, and then he frowned. "Any idea why they tried to kill me, Sam?"

The marshal slowed to a stop and rubbed his chin, studying his deputies. "I guess the excitement's over for the night," he told them. "Go on home and get a good night's sleep. Gabe, you stay on a minute."

The blond man shifted his weight a little and said, "Uh, there's one other thing, sir. I've known Steve for a bit and I can't see him killin' a helpless man."

"He was there," said McClure. "You heard what happened."

"Yeah, I heard." The deputy looked at his boots, shuffling one of them in the dirt. "But he didn't have to *know*. He didn't have to be downstairs. I was watchin' him and he looked kind o' scared when you started talkin' about the lump on Mr. McClure's head."

McClure nodded, looking thoughtful. "Maybe 'cause he knew the sheriff was downstairs before we come in."

"Then he could help us, couldn't he?"

"He'd be turnin' on his own boss," McClure said doubtfully.

"I still don't think he wants any part of a killing."

"Then talk to him, Jim."

"Yes sir!"

"Get him alone tomorrow and scare him a little. Tell him it's true, what I said. We're gonna put Thorne in jail along with anyone who helps him. Then see if ol' Steve feels like tellin' a judge what he saw. It'll be important evidence."

"Yes *sir*," said Jim. He lifted his chin a little higher and strode away. The other two deputies went more reluctantly, glancing repeatedly at Gabe as if they wondered why he enjoyed the privilege of staying behind. After they had gone McClure started walking again, moving toward the warehouses and corrals on the edge of town.

"I think they were getting scared," he told the rancher. "That's why they tried to kill you. They couldn't let you get to trial Friday because they weren't sure they had the evidence they needed." McClure frowned. "And when I say 'they' I really mean Chester Tomlin, Frank. It looks like this has been his doing from start to finish."

"That part I already figured out," Haywood said impatiently. "The son of a bitch bought a quarter section out from under me. Then he used the deed to make it look like I stole his wife."

The marshal was nodding. "Gabe thinks the real idea— and I have to say I agree with him—what Tomlin really wanted was to get rid of his wife completely. Make it look like she was in danger and then have her killed, so Tomlin could inherit her money."

McClure went on to describe the extent of the storekeeper's business ventures in Sidney, surprising Haywood as much as Gabe had surprised Sarah. He also told the rancher about the shootout of the night before, and Gabe's escape with Jane Tomlin.

"Five men," said Haywood, looking at Gabe with new respect.

"It was supposed to look like you'd hired them, too," said McClure, describing the note that one of the gunmen had in his pockets.

"But Mrs. Tomlin told her husband about her suspicions before we left," said Gabe. "I think that's why he got scared enough to want you killed. He had no way of knowing who she'd talk to."

"Is Mrs. Tomlin safe?" said Haywood.

Gabe bowed his head to hide a smile.

"She's staying with one of my deputies," said McClure. "But Tomlin is still trying to find her and it might give us a chance to trap him." The marshal told his friend about the offer of a bribe to Sarah Prater. "If Tomlin tries to kill his wife or get her back, you see—if he attacks the place we tell Sarah to tell him—then it'll prove that he's the one. The judge will have to let you go."

"You really think he'll try again?" said Haywood. "The little bastard has already gone through half a dozen men."

The marshal waved his hand. "A dozen more just like them come through here every day," he said. "A gold rush draws the worst types along with some of the best."

"It could be quite a battle," said the rancher.

McClure frowned and said, "Don't I know it. But right now it seems like the best way to prove what Tomlin's up to. Everything else is just guesswork because he's been too clever to leave many tracks."

"Maybe he got too clever for his own good," Haywood suggested. "Maybe he'll trip over his own feet. Most men don't go to all that trouble just to get rid of their wives."

"But she wasn't the only target," said Gabe.

The rancher and the marshal glanced at each other. "You're talking about me," said Haywood.

Gabe nodded. "Seems like he wanted you to hang."

"That's the part that don't make any sense," Haywood said slowly. "Are you sayin' you know what Tomlin has against me?"

"I think so." Gabe's eyes glinted with humor. "I'd say he found out that you and his wife were in love. It probably didn't make him too happy."

McClure and Haywood glanced at each other again. Then the rancher glowered at Gabe.

"Don't worry," Gabe assured him. "Your secret's safe with me. As a matter of fact I think it solves another problem."

"Which one?" McClure snapped.

Gabe looked at the marshal. "You have to hide him out somewhere, don't you? Keep him safe from Thorne and Tomlin?"

McClure nodded.

"Well, you've already got one deputy tied up that way. Why waste your manpower when you can have the same deputy guarding two people."

McClure was the first to get it. His old grey eyes lit up and he said, "Sure, that makes all the sense in the world."

"What?" said Haywood. "What makes sense?"

"Gabe is sayin' I should put you and Mrs. Tomlin together," said McClure. "Have you stay in the same house."

"Well I'll be damned," said the rancher, grinning at Gabe. "I sure like the way you think."

CHAPTER THIRTEEN

At dawn Gabe was standing in the cold clear water of Lodgepole Creek, just south of Sidney. He could see the town in the distance beyond the grassy bank, a small huddle of buildings surrounded by an endless stretch of land. In all that emptiness there was no hint that life might exist anywhere else. Gabe looked out at the horizon and felt as if he was seeing the emptiness inside his heart. At first he didn't understand what it meant, or why he started thinking about Frank Haywood and Jane Tomlin.

There had been a lot of joy when the two of them were brought together in the home of the marshal's deputy, Nate Brandon. McClure had asked Mrs. Brandon to wake the woman at once so he could tell her what had happened. Jane Tomlin had been frightened when she heard the story of Haywood's brush with death, but when she understood that he was free of Thorne—and that there was no more reason to hide her feelings from the others in the room—she had rushed to throw her arms around Haywood's neck. He had laughed and picked her up in his arms, whirling her around in a full circle with her nightgown and robe trailing out behind her. Gabe remembered the happiness on each of their faces as they turned. It transformed them, giving the woman a soft-eyed beauty that stirred Gabe's blood while Haywood's grin was aglow with good-natured humor.

Deputy Brandon's wife had clapped her hands together and joined in the laughter, going to stand at her husband's side. They had put their arms around each other as they watched. The marshal had looked on with equal pleasure, tempered by a depth of sadness that misted his eyes.

Gabe wondered if McClure's sadness was like the thing he himself was feeling now, as he stood in the creek. It seemed to be a hunger or an ache that had settled in his heart.

Gabe had finally returned to Sarah's shack at three o'clock in the morning, stirred by everything he'd seen. Nor was he disappointed. The woman had come awake with hungers of her own, and for a time the two of them were like raging prairie fires joined together, consuming everything in their path. Finally they had burned themselves out. They were lying together, fully spent, when Gabe looked through the window high above them and saw the first touch of grey in the sky.

He had left the woman almost immediately, coming to the creek to begin preparing himself for the battle he expected that night.

Gabe still followed most of the Lakota customs. For a while it had been a matter of habit, a fear of turning his back on everything the Oglalas drummed into him during his childhood. Later he had been tempted by the easier ways of the whites, who didn't follow nearly so many rituals. But in the end he had come to prefer the old customs. He believed there was purpose and harmony in each one.

His first step that morning, for example, was to wash his

private parts in the cold water. An Oglala warrior would have been nervous about fighting after he had been with a woman. Young boys were even told there was a danger of going blind if they touched a sacred pipe afterwards, unless they'd already washed themselves. That part made Gabe smile, but he knew the ritual cleansing helped to clear his mind. It made him work harder at leaving the pleasures of the night behind, so he could prepare himself for the harsher events that lay ahead.

When Gabe came out of the creek, however, he knew that washing would not be enough this time. The emptiness was still there inside. The difference was that now he recognized it as something he'd felt before. He also realized that Sarah had already explained it to him, in a way, when she said that a man wants a woman to want him. He'd turned it into a joke with her, but now he understood that the thing they felt toward each other was not as good as the thing between Frank Haywood and Jane Tomlin. It left him with a hollow feeling, which made his spirit weak. He would have to purify his spirit as well as his body.

Gabe led his pony down the creek until he lost sight of the town, then built a fire on a level piece of ground near the water. He collected several stones, choosing them carefully to make sure they wouldn't explode in the fire. While they heated he cut fourteen willow branches along the creek and lashed them into a domed framework, centered above a shallow pit. He cut sage plants to make a sitting place beneath the frame. He left a canteen beside the sage, then covered the dome with a blanket from his bedroll.

Gabe followed the ways he'd been taught as closely as he could: the laying of wood for the fire, the placement of the pit, the shape of the dome. All was performed in the sacred manner. In the old days, his spiritual advisers had believed that the use of trade goods like canteens and blankets would displease the spirits. But the coming of the whites had changed everything.

Gabe used a pair of sticks to carry the heated stones inside, placing them in the shallow pit in the arrangement representing the four Great Directions. Finally he stripped off his clothing and closed himself inside the lodge. The blackness was so perfect that after a while he could see a faint glow from the pit. He splashed water on his face and hair, then sprinkled it on the stones.

There was a crack like a rifle shot as steam hissed up through the small closed space, stinging Gabe's flesh and searing his lungs. Sweat poured off his face and blinded him. He remembered Haywood clawing at the sheet around his neck, knowing better now how it must have felt.

The steam choked Gabe and prickled his skin until the lodge was almost unbearable, but he endured and there was a clean pleasure in the knowledge of his endurance. Three more times he sprinkled water over the rocks, praying to his own helper spirits and asking them for power. He felt the steam cleansing the inside of his body and purifying his *ni*, which the whites might have called his spirit. He wasn't sure if that was really the same thing, but he was pretty sure that the whites didn't worry much about whether they felt it inside them. For Gabe it was the same thing as his own life, the power of the life that went through him each time he breathed. Everything he did in his rituals, he knew, was aimed at *feeling* that power—at believing in it and making it greater.

When he was through Gabe came out of the purification lodge and rubbed sage over his body, then bathed again in the creek. Afterward he sat before the remains of the fire and filled the bowl of his pipe with willow bark tobacco. Now that he had cleansed his own spirit it was time to speak to the other powers in the world.

He addressed them by presenting his pipe to the four Great Directions, holding it first to the West, followed by the North, East and South. He made sure to grip the bowl of the pipe in his left hand, the stem in his right. He held the pipe down toward the earth, mother of all life, then up toward the sky, representing the mysterious, unknown power that made all things. This was *Wakan-tanka*.

Now when Gabe put the pipe to his mouth, he thought of the smoke as the power of other spirits. He felt them entering his body. He wasn't sure he believed anymore that this was really happening, maybe, but he did believe that he had renewed his contact with the great natural forces in the world. It was easy to lose track of them in a town, but now he saw the sun with new eyes and listened to the wind with new ears. The emptiness of the morning had been replaced by the fullness of his own power as well as a sense of his place in the universe. He had pleased the spirits with the care of his preparations and he knew they would lend him their help.

They might even speak to him, if necessary. There was no time to seek a vision, but Gabe was feeling the need for rest. He found a growth of cottonwood trees dense enough to hide his pony, and stretched out in the soft grass. Before he slept he reminded himself to pay attention to any dreams the spirits might send his way.

Sarah Prater frowned when she first saw the house Chester Tomlin had told her to come to. For one thing, she knew from Gabe that it wasn't Tomlin's home. For another, she thought there should have been a light in some of the windows. It was early evening and the sun had gone down far enough to fill the streets of Sidney with a gloomy afterglow. It was also late enough that Tomlin should have closed his store already and finished his supper. As she turned in at a rusty iron gate Sarah began to worry that Tomlin had changed his mind about their arrangement, or learned what he wanted to know from someone else. In either case it would mean the loss of five thousand dollars.

She had been hungering for the money ever since Tomlin made the offer, counting on it to provide her a life of ease for a while. Perhaps even a life without men. It wasn't that Sarah didn't want men. The problem was that most of them were such sorry specimens. Only rarely did a man excite her deeply. But when one of them did it just made things worse for her, because the kind of men who met her needs weren't likely to stay for long.

That's the way it was with Gabe. If she allowed herself she knew she would hunger for the chance to spend the rest of her life with him. She would trade the money without a second thought. All the money in the world, for that matter. But she pushed the longing away because she knew it was just a matter of time before he left. The same restless spirit that excited her would drive him on, and she would be lost. This knowledge—almost an instinct—allowed her to lessen the coming sorrow by enjoying Gabe without letting him become important to her. It was not enough, but it was all she had.

Sarah studied the dark house for a moment, then took a deep breath and walked up the front steps to the porch. There was an oval window of frosted glass in the front door. A shadow fell across the window before Sarah could knock and a second later Chester Tomlin opened the door. A smile appeared fleetingly on his face, but Sarah's lasting impression was one of harrowed, sleepless eyes.

"Come in, come in," said Tomlin. "You have news?"

"I wasn't even sure you were here," said Sarah, looking over his shoulder. "Where's your furniture? Why don't you have any lights burning?"

Tomlin opened the door wide and stood back, allowing her to pass. "No one lives here, Miss Prater. This house is only one of my investments. I thought it wise to be discreet about our arrangement."

Sarah nodded and said, *"Your* investments?"

"Well of course I mean ours." Tomlin was closing the door behind him. "Mrs. Tomlin and I had a great deal of faith in the future of Sidney, which we backed with money. But I imagine you've already heard about that from Mr. Conrad."

He was watching her with a look of shrewd appraisal that surprised and troubled her, although neither emotion showed in her expression. She warned herself to be more careful but the only thing Tomlin saw was an amused, enigmatic smile.

"That's right," she told him. "I've heard at least one story, anyway."

Anger flared in Tomlin's eyes. "I'll bet you've heard plenty of stories," he said. "Those two are making fools of us!"

Sarah frowned. "Are you sure, Mr. Tomlin? Gabe insisted he had no interest in your wife."

"Only because he wants your help, don't you see? He wants a place to hide. Pretty soon he'll be asking for railroad tickets and things like that. I guarantee it!" Tomlin cleared his throat, recovering himself, then glanced around the room with an apologetic look. "Please pardon the accommodations, by the way. Our business shouldn't take very long."

They were standing in the parlor because there was no place to sit. The room was bare, with no rug on the floor and only thin lace curtains to filter the dim light coming through the windows.

"Then all you want to do is get your wife back?" said Sarah.

"That would please me very much."

"What about Frank Haywood. I hear he's not in the jail any longer."

"That man!" Tomlin sputtered. "If McClure lets him disappear I'll make sure he—"

"I know where he is."

"Haywood too?" said the storekeeper. He was staring up at Sarah, blinking furiously. "Where?"

"I think that's worth more, don't you?"

"Seven thousand dollars is a lot of money, Miss Prater."

"But it's all I'll ever get." Sarah fixed him with a pointed look. *"You'll* have your wife's inheritance."

"It does have its limits, you know."

"Oh, I'm sorry," said Sarah. "Then I guess you're not interested." She turned toward the door.

"All right!" Tomlin snapped. "You've called my bluff. You have the upper hand and you know it."

Sarah grinned. "I won't make it too painful, Mr. Tomlin. How about an even ten thousand dollars for the two of them?"

Tomlin nodded. "But I still only have five thousand right now. I can give you the rest later, after I have my wife back."

Sarah's look of disappointment was real. She sensed that Tomlin was telling the truth and realized she would never see the rest of the money. "Score this one for you," she said. "I guess I don't have any choice." Then she shrugged, eyeing the storekeeper. "You would have found both of them anyway, since Marshal McClure is keeping them in the same place."

Sarah was not at all disappointed with the storekeeper's reaction. The thought of his wife together with the rancher made his jaw drop open as if he'd been punched in the stomach. "The bastard!" he said. Then he looked at Sarah.

"Forgive me. I mean McClure, of course. For putting Jane near the very man who's caused her so much pain."

Sarah nodded, seeing a crafty look come into the storekeeper's eyes.

"On the other hand," he said, "it does make things easier, doesn't it?"

"I thought so."

"And where is this place?"

"Where's the five thousand dollars?"

Tomlin smiled. Sarah shivered.

"In the back," said the storekeeper. "Come with me."

He led the way through a dining room and into the kitchen, where he took a cloth-wrapped bundle out of a drawer. He unwrapped it on the counter near the sink. Fifty-dollar notes spilled out of the bundle, matching the greenbacks Tomlin had given Sarah the previous day. She was sure they were the remains of the ransom for his wife, after he'd finished paying off the men Gabe had already killed.

Sarah stared at the pile of greenbacks and felt a dryness in her throat. "You know the old warehouse that Post and Stearns used to have? Out at the end of Lincoln Street?"

Tomlin was looking thoughtful. "Sure," he said. "It's still empty, isn't it?"

"I guess it was." Sarah licked her lips. "But that's where the marshal is hiding your wife and Mr. Haywood."

"Strange place, don't you think?"

Sarah frowned, tearing her eyes away from the money on the counter. "I don't see why, Mr. Tomlin. Gabe said it was easier to defend, since the building is kind of off by itself."

"It *is* guarded, then."

"I'm afraid so."

"And I'm surprised," said Tomlin, still watching Sarah.

"I would have bet that Jane was being kept by one of McClure's deputies. Fellow by the name of Brandon."

Sarah fought to keep any expression from showing on her face. "Brandon?" she said. "A deputy? What makes you think so."

"Because no one's seen him on patrol since the night before last. It seemed like more than just a coincidence."

Sarah frowned and bent over the counter, gathering up the notes. "Gabe might have been lying to me," she said. "Or maybe Brandon's been in the warehouse all this time?"

"Perhaps," said Tomlin.

Sarah was having trouble breathing. She kept stacking the money while she forced an airy tone. "Anything's possible, I guess."

"But you're sure it's the warehouse?"

"That's what Gabe told me this morning. And I think he trusted me." She re-wrapped the money in the cloth and stuffed it into her purse.

"I'd rather you stay a while longer," said Tomlin.

When Sarah turned around there was a small revolver in his fist. She'd been getting ready to insist on leaving the house but now she only stared at the gun in silence, her mouth still hanging open.

"Actually it's a lady's model," said the storekeeper. "Something you might want to consider yourself someday. Because .25 caliber can be just as deadly at this range."

"But I just want to go home," Sarah said. "I gave you what you wanted."

"I hope so. I'm sure you did. But it makes me a little nervous that you took all your money out of the bank today."

Sarah shivered again and glanced toward the front parlor. There was a street just outside, lined by other homes with people inside them.

"Don't," Tomlin warned.

Sarah jumped at the harsh sound of his voice, turning back to find something new in his expression. It was a flat, cold look that left her even more frightened than before.

"I'll use this if I have to," Tomlin said. "No one knows you're here. They'd never even find your body. So just relax until I find out whether you've really earned that money."

"But I have!"

"Then you'll be free in the morning." Tomlin took the purse out of her hand and pointed the gun toward a door on his right. "For tonight, however, I've prepared a comfortable place for you in the cellar."

Sarah hesitated, eyeing the distance between them. Tomlin gave her a cool smile and stepped back, gesturing again with the revolver. She opened the door and went down into a musty room full of stale air. A pair of lanterns was already burning, which made Sarah examine the walls. There were no windows in any of them.

Beneath the stairs she saw an old mattress with a coil of rope on top. She turned on Tomlin in a flash of panic but he raised the pistol between them, staring at her with the most cold-blooded look she'd ever seen. Even through her fear she recognized that he would kill her as easily as he had said he would—that he would have no hesitation about pulling the trigger. She allowed him to tie her down with legs and arms outspread, the rope running under the mattress between her ankles and wrists. Sarah's helplessness made her feel a little numb as she watched the storekeeper run up to close the door at the top of the steps.

When he came back he was smiling, holding the gun in one hand and her purse in the other. He put them both on one of the steps above Sarah's head and stood looking down at her.

"Exquisite," he said, letting out a long sigh. "If you only knew how much I've dreamed of this."

Sarah lost any hope she might have had. Her eyes brimmed with fear.

"Don't waste your breath," said Tomlin, nodding toward the walls. "Solid stone all around." He kneeled beside the mattress and tore Sarah's dress off her shoulders, then stared at her breasts as they rose and fell with her labored breathing. He pulled out a handkerchief to mop his glistening forehead. "Oh, Lord," he said. "You know one reason I wanted to become the most powerful man in Sidney?"

Sarah shook her head.

"Because I thought maybe then you'd notice me." Tomlin grinned like a shy boy, still kneeling beside her. In the next instant his eyes turned cold. "Go ahead and laugh if you wish. I know how foolish I seem. A man like me learns he has to pay for everything he wants."

The storekeeper put the handkerchief away and, after a moment's hesitation, he began to squeeze Sarah's breasts. As if he'd been working up the courage. His eyes fluttered and he ran his hands down the length of her body, flinging her dress up over her thighs. Again he stopped to savor what he saw. Then he began to take off his own clothes.

"The way I see it," he said, "ten thousand dollars buys me a lot. And we have a long night ahead."

Gabe woke up in time to see the sun hanging on the far rim of the prairie. He sat and watched it disappear, smelling the grass beneath him while the night breezes touched his skin. There had been no dreams he could remember but he still felt the sharpness of his senses, the clarity and harmony that gave him a knowledge of his own power.

Gabe went to his pony and untied the Winchester carbine which Tomlin had given him on his first day in Sidney. Anything built that complicated made him nervous—the more moving parts, he thought, the more there was to go wrong—but Tomlin had kept reassuring him of the weapon's reputation for reliability. Gabe worked the lever a few times and liked the smooth feel of it. He dug some .44 shells out of a case and pushed them one at a time into the side port, loading up the tube under the barrel. Then he sighted on a branch fifty yards away and squeezed the trigger.

The first shot was a miss, but he was ready for another try with a flick of his wrist, almost before he knew what he'd done. He looked down at the rifle and grinned, thinking of the time it would have taken to shove another paper cartridge into his Sharps. It wasn't easy to change old habits, but Gabe had to admit he was getting excited by the possibilities of the Winchester. He shot off the rest of the tube within a matter of seconds, just as quickly finding the carbine's aim. He settled it into his scabbard and tied the Sharps on the back of the saddle.

Exchanging the Remingtons for Tomlin's Colt would have to wait, however. Gabe decided that familiarity was more important when it came to fast work and snap shots with a revolver. Gabe broke out the powder and ball and began to recharge the chambers, putting fresh caps over the nipples. He did the same for his two spare cylinders, which could be just as affected by vibration and moisture.

Then it was time to go and spring the trap. As the twilight faded Gabe unwrapped his bedroll and pulled out the long coat Tomlin had seen on that first day. Gabe had made it himself from a single buffalo hide, although the yellow symbol on the back had been painted by his mother when the hide was still part of her tipi cover. Then Captain Price had killed her during a cavalry attack and the soldiers had destroyed the camp, throwing food and lodge skins onto great bonfires. Gabe had found the hide afterward, somehow untouched by the fire.

The coat had many meanings for Gabe. It helped him keep

the memory of his mother alive, as well as the happiness and sense of safety he had known as a child in her lodge. But there was also the yellow symbol. It represented *Wakinyan*, the Winged God that was also known by the whites as the Thunder Bird. *Wakinyan* was the Lakota patron of ferocity and courage who had appeared in Gabe's first vision a few days before his mother's death, coming out of the sky to settle about his shoulders in a protective way. The Winged God had thus become a powerful part of his medicine. The preservation of the *Wakinyan* symbol in the fire was just one more sign of its power.

Gabe slipped the coat over his shoulders, feeling that he had cloaked himself with the power of his patron spirit of battle.

CHAPTER FOURTEEN

Sam McClure was joined by two of the three deputies Gabe had met the night before, leaving one to make the rounds in town. The marshal had also lined up two of his men who normally would have been home sleeping, along with four old friends of Frank Haywood's who were eager to join the fight. Each man had been told to slip into the Post and Stearns warehouse by himself, just after full dark, where the marshal gathered them around a low-trimmed lantern for a final conference.

"I'm sure we'll see action before dawn," said McClure. Even held to a whisper, his voice echoed through the dark and empty length of the warehouse. "Judge Wilcox is on tonight's train and plannin' to hold court tomorrow morning at eight. He's deciding whether to send Frank to trial. Chester Tomlin can't afford to let his wife testify."

One of the deputies looked puzzled. "What would she say, marshal?"

A couple of Haywood's friends glanced at each other and

one of them winked, but McClure was looking at the floor and chewing the inside of his lip. "Let's see if it comes to that," he finally answered. "I'd much rather show the judge a hired tough who'll say that Tomlin did the hiring."

"So we have to take them alive?" said one of the rancher's friends.

McClure nodded. "But don't risk anything," he said. "I mean I'd *like* that, but the attack by itself will be enough to show what Tomlin's up to."

"But what if we're not facing a gang of toughs?" said the same man. "What if Tomlin has the sheriff send his own men to get his prisoner back?"

"I think the sheriff's gettin' too nervous for that," said McClure, pointing his chin at the blond-haired boy with the missing tooth. "Jim here has one of Thorne's deputies tucked away in our holding cell. Some of you know Steve Shlisky?"

There was a nodding of heads in the flickering lamplight.

"Well, Steve's been telling us that Thorne got pretty worked up after we took Frank out of the jail last night. Kept threatening the kid, tellin' him to forget anything he saw."

"What *did* he see?"

"Pretty much what we figured. Thorne come runnin' up the stairs about the same time our lookout blew the whistle."

"Son of a bitch!" said the volunteer, echoed by a bitter chorus of agreement.

"Steve's smart enough to know what happened," McClure said. "And smart enough to see that his boss is backing a loser. He don't want no part of it. He's willin' to talk and my guess is that Thorne already knows he's missing." The marshal shook his head. "No, he won't make things worse for himself. We'll be facing a bunch of drifters tonight and nothing more."

"That's fine with me," said the volunteer. "The bastards are gonna be sorry."

But by five o'clock the next morning, after more than eight hours of waiting, Gabe was having his doubts. The force of ten lawmen and volunteers had filtered out of the warehouse the same way they'd gone in, quietly and one at a time. They had formed a ring around the building, taking up positions mapped out for them by McClure. The marshal was sure they would not be seen, since Sarah's meeting with Tomlin had been scheduled for less than half an hour before the conference around the lantern.

Yet dawn was about to break and nothing had happened, and Gabe was feeling uneasy. Perhaps he and the marshal had overlooked something in their plans. It alarmed Gabe to see the first touch of blue-black light in the sky, slowly erasing the glitter of stars. He knew the sun would be coming up soon, making their trap useless.

That started him thinking about the night before, when he watched the sun go down. He remembered the way it grew in size as it settled toward the rim of the world, losing the shape of its circle and melting into the prairie like liquid fire.

The picture stayed in his mind and seemed to take it over. Gabe blinked. He was seeing the dark shape of the warehouse that loomed up before him, but over the top of it he still saw the fiery sun. It was there on its own, as in a vision, and soon it began to spread itself across the sky. The sun grew into a wall of flames so brilliant that Gabe could almost feel its heat. He was wide-eyed now, staring into the fire in his vision. He thought he saw the outline of a house at its center, with flames curling up the sides.

Gabe crawled out of his nest in a stack of railroad ties and ran toward the tool shed where McClure was standing watch. In his moccasins he moved as silently as a ghost, calling out a low warning before he slipped through the door. He stopped just inside, unable to see anything except the outline of a small window. Then McClure's harsh whisper jumped at him from the darkness.

"Who the hell told you to move?" said the marshal. "What if someone saw you?"

"No one's watching," said Gabe. "Because no one's coming. They would have attacked by now."

"They *have* to come. Wilcox holds court in less than three hours."

"What if we're watching the wrong trap?"

"It's the only one there is."

"I wonder," said Gabe. "Hasn't Brandon stayed home with Mrs. Tomlin since the night I delivered her?"

The marshal's form was visible now in front of the window. It moved a little and Gabe realized McClure was nodding. "But I put out the word that Brandon's sick," he said. "Everyone thinks he's got a stomach ailment."

"What if Tomlin doesn't believe it?"

The marshal was silent for a moment and Gabe tried in vain to see his expression. Then McClure sighed and said, "Let's not get too clever for our own good, Gabe. I've made my choice and I'm sticking with it."

"What if you're wrong?"

"What if *you're* wrong! Those bastards could be waiting for the first crack of twilight to show them the way. You know how spooky everything looks about then."

Gabe turned to go, feeling a sudden sense of urgency.

"Get back here!" the marshal rasped. "I don't want my forces split."

"I'm only one man, Mr. McClure. You have eight more besides yourself."

"You'll give away our position."

"Don't worry."

"I'm *ordering* you to stay."

Gabe pulled the tin star off his shirt and held it out. "That's why I don't like these things," he said. "I guess you can have it back."

"Now listen—"

"No time," said Gabe. He crouched near the door, laying the star on the ground before he disappeared through the opening.

"Goddamn it, Gabe, get back here before I—"

But the marshal's whispered threats were lost on Gabe as soon as he ran from the shed. McClure had chosen the Post and Stearns building because Nate Brandon's house was on the other side of Sidney. Now it seemed impossibly far away. Gabe changed course, deciding to satisfy himself that Sarah was safe and maybe learn something about Tomlin's reaction to her story.

What he found was the thing he hadn't let himself think about. He burst into Sarah's empty shanty and stood in the middle of the floor, staring at her bed while he cursed bitterly under his breath. Then he stepped back into the night and sniffed the air. A drifting bite of smoke teased his senses. Once more he broke into a run, holding the Winchester down against his leg. The smell of smoke grew stronger, and then he could see traces of it against the remaining stars.

Gabe called on his memories of the Brandon house as he ran, seeing the way it sat on a corner lot. He realized that the front entrance was exposed on two sides, while no one could leave through the back door without being seen from one of the streets. Gabe tried to remember what the streets looked like, thinking about where he'd place himself if he was trying to lay an ambush.

The business center was far behind when he saw an orange glow two blocks down, about where Brandon's house should be. He levered a shell into the chamber of his Winchester and ran even faster along the edge of the street. He still moved noiselessly—the Oglala training of his childhood made that much automatic—but there were no awnings here to cast concealing shadows. All he saw were low fences around small yards with hardly any trees.

But there was no more time for being careful. The orange glow burned brighter up the street and shimmered through the heavy smoke billowing above the neighboring homes. Gabe was just reaching the last corner when an explosion of gunfire beat against his ears. He saw one muzzle blast behind a picket fence on his left and took the fence at a run, leaping over sharp points of wood to land in a yard across the street from the Brandon house.

Gabe almost tripped over a man lying on his belly, watching through a knothole in the fence while he worked the lever of a carbine. The man sensed something wrong and looked up in time to see Gabe's Winchester slashing down. The heavy steel barrel caught him across the forehead, bringing a burst of blood before the man's body collapsed over his rifle.

Gabe glanced across the fence at the flames engulfing Brandon's home. They were climbing up the sides instead of coming out through the windows. Brandon himself was out front, holding his leg and limping back toward the open door. His wife watched through the opening, trying to reach out for him while the light from the fire caught the anguish in her face. It also showed that a woman's arms were holding her back. Gabe thought, *Good work, Jane.*

In the next instant he saw the flames reflecting on a rifle barrel rising up by her side. The muzzle pointed straight at Gabe and he ducked, rolling away behind the fence. He found himself on his back and looking up at another man sighting down from the porch only a few feet behind him. A shot crashed out of the burning house and the man wavered, then held steady. But by then Gabe had pivoted his Winchester into place. He pulled the trigger with the butt against his hip. The man on the porch let out a gurgling scream and dropped his gun to grab his neck.

He was still falling when a small barrage of slugs ripped through the fence boards, showering Gabe with splinters as he rolled again and worked the lever. He jumped up a few feet from where he'd gone down and threw the rifle to his shoulder while he sought a target. A puff of smoke was drifting from a porch across the corner. Gabe shot into the shadow at its source, then started running as the assassin staggered out into the open and fell.

A split second passed while the other bushwhackers reloaded and then Gabe was drawing a new round of fire. There was a tug at his long coat and a flash straight ahead, behind the tree he was running for on the other side of the street. Gabe's left hand was already reaching instinctively for the pistol under his arm while he weaved out to the side. When the outlaw popped out to try another shot Gabe wasn't where he was supposed to be and the outlaw found himself more exposed than he meant to be. Gabe shot him in the belly and kicked the gun out of his hand when he reached the tree.

Gabe guessed there were five shooters remaining and maybe more around the other side of the Brandon house. He put the revolver away and sheltered himself behind the tree, ignoring the man writhing in agony at his feet. Gabe held the bead of his Winchester on the corner of a building where he'd seen another flash. A man eased out far enough to take aim and Gabe's bullet tore through his one open eye. There was another volley and then the echoes rolled away beneath the snapping of the flames.

"Listen to me!" Gabe called out. "You've lost this fight. Four are dead already and one will go to prison."

Gabe would try anything to improve his odds. He heard a

shot and the chunk of a slug burying itself in the tree. Gabe scowled.

"You're only showing yourself for fools," he yelled. "The marshal is on his way with eight men. Do you want him to catch you here? Is it worth the money?"

Gabe waited a few seconds, listening to the crackle of the fire and feeling its heat against his face. Then he pushed off from the tree and ran toward the house. This time there were only three shots, one of them whistling past his ear. It made him grateful for the protection of the Winged God.

Once he reached the far corner he was safe, since he'd cut down the men who were watching that side of the house. He drew fire again from the other street as he sprinted for the back door, yelling his name as he went through. He found Frank Haywood and Nate Brandon just inside, huddled against the searing heat with their arms around the women. They were waiting for help but the fire was fast closing in around them. Jane Tomlin was trying to hide her fear while the deputy's wife watched the destruction of her home with tears streaming down her cheeks.

"There's a way out," Gabe shouted over the roar of the fire. "But we have to go *now*, before they shift positions. I'll give you cover."

The deputy's eyes swept over Gabe's coat with a skeptical look but Haywood was eyeing the fire. "No choice," he yelled. "We have to try."

Gabe was digging shells out of his pocket and stuffing them into the Winchester. He handed it to the rancher, then pulled the Remingtons from his belt and shoulder holster. "You have to get around the side of the house I just came from," he said. "After that you cut *away* from the corner and go like hell toward town until you run into McClure and his men. They must be almost here by now."

"Where will you be?" said Haywood.

"I've got other business," Gabe said grimly. "But no more talk. It's time to move."

Brandon took a step toward the door and stumbled, grabbing one leg and crying out in pain. Gabe saw that his trousers were soaked with blood.

"Help him," Haywood told the women. "Each of you take an arm over your shoulders and follow me."

When they were ready Gabe jumped through the door and let loose with the Remingtons as fast as he could pull the trigger. Ear the hammers back and squeeze, first the right and then the left and then the right again. Nine shots in less than nine seconds, his own smoke stinging his eyes. He crouched beneath it in the Brandon's back yard and aimed for movement or muzzle flashes, trying just to keep heads down while Haywood led the women and the deputy toward the safe side of the burning house. Then Gabe backed away to the corner and followed them to the street, using the moment of shelter to replace his empty cylinders.

From the side of the house he weaved back to the cottonwood in front, stepping over the body sprawled across its roots. At a signal from the rancher Gabe laid down another round of cover fire while Haywood led the retreat. Two ambushers ran around the corner for a last clear shot and paid for it with their lives. They were also the last ones Gabe saw. Haywood and Brandon had disappeared with the women down the street and if any of the attackers were left, they were disappearing in the opposite direction.

Chester Tomlin held his breath when he heard the first roll of Gabe's cover fire, then grinned at Sarah when he heard the second. It was a grin that made her wish she could gouge his eyes with her fingers.

"That's it," Tomlin chortled in the silence that followed. "They're all finished now."

Sarah looked up at him in horror when he laughed and started moving inside her again, closing his eyes with that terrible grin still on his face. She tried to shrink away from him but the ropes held her in place while he grunted and pumped even harder, his breath coming faster until a spasm shook his body.

It was the fourth time he had climbed on top of her during the night. Each time he would squeeze her too hard and sometimes she would cry until he had satisfied himself. Then he would sleep for a while, only to wake up with a renewed desire. This time he had just been getting started when the sound of the first shots drifted faintly through the stone walls of the basement. The sound excited him and he beat himself harder against Sarah's body. This time she didn't feel it as much, however. The fear of what was happening outside had numbed her to the pain.

Now he lay on top of her with his puffy, sweating face against her breasts. He twisted his neck for a sideways glance, laughing when he saw the look of hope in her eyes.

"I'll bet you think that was McClure and his men," he said. "But think harder, my dear. We never would have heard that all the way from the warehouse." The glitter in his eyes was as sharp as the edge in his voice. "No, what we heard was the end of Frank Haywood and my sweet wife."

Sarah stared at him with a new sense of desolation. The little man knew. He knew everything and maybe he was right about the rancher and Jane Tomlin being dead. It also meant he would kill her. She jumped when he laughed again.

"I wonder whether they shot the bitch down," said Tomlin. "Or maybe she let herself get burned to death." He laughed with pleasure, then gave Sarah a cold look. "Just as long as she knew it was my doing before she died."

Sarah found it hard to believe what she was hearing. Even after all her bad luck with men she hadn't thought one of them could be this twisted. Tomlin was eyeing her, apparently failing to understand her expression.

"You're surprised?" he said. "You really thought I'd believe your story about the warehouse." He shook his head. "You're just like everyone else!" he yelled in a sudden rage. "You all think I'm stupid, don't you? Just because a man looks like me he must be simple." The rage disappeared as suddenly as it came. He gave Sarah a conspiratorial wink and said, "But that's fine with me. It lets me do things, right? People can look right at me and never see me."

Tomlin laughed and pushed himself off her body. When he was standing he looked down at it with a longing, wistful glance. "Ah, it's a shame," he said, sighing as he reached for the little revolver on the step. Then he giggled. "But I do have a large inheritance to collect, don't I? I'd better go and change so I can look my best for court."

Tomlin bent down to hold the muzzle of the revolver against the bridge of her nose while he cocked the hammer. Sarah squeezed her eyes shut for a moment and then forced them open. She opened them as wide as she could, staring up at the storekeeper. He began to frown. After a moment he pulled the gun away.

"No, I might spoil my breakfast," said Tomlin. "The idea of such a terrible waste." Then he grinned, looking at her breasts again. "Besides, I want to get in a lot more fucking."

CHAPTER FIFTEEN

Gabe frowned at the still form stretched out behind the picket fence, worrying that the blow from his rifle had been too hard. Then he saw the steady rise and fall of the man's breathing. Even across the street there was plenty of light from the fire.

Gabe lifted the body onto his shoulder and walked away from the burning house. After he'd gone a block or so he heard running footsteps and excited voices in the distance. He ducked into a side street and kept going, wanting to keep his prize to himself for a while.

He knew people were watching from some of the homes, awakened by the shots but afraid to go out. He turned down the first alley he came to, in a section where the homeowners could afford carriage houses in back. He found an empty one with an open door and went inside, dumping the assassin's body onto the ground.

The man rolled against Gabe's legs, reaching for the

revolver still in his holster. Gabe took a hard fall on his back but managed to kick up at the man's wrist. The gun went flying and the man yelled, lashing out with his boot. Gabe felt it graze his head as he twisted away and onto his feet. The two of them stood staring at each other for a moment, the killer holding his arm and blinking against the fresh blood that poured from the gash on his forehead. He tried to run but Gabe was on him in a second, knocking him down and landing with his knees in the small of the man's back.

"Jesus Christ!" said Gabe. "Don't you want a chance to stay alive?"

"Fuck you," said the killer. He had long glistening black hair that flowed down over his collar. "Let me up or I'll kill you."

Gabe laughed harshly, twisting the man's arm up between his shoulder blades. "Just tell me who hired you scum. That's all I want."

"A big guy. His name was Haywood."

Gabe twisted the arm up higher and the man's face clenched in pain.

"Wrong answer," said Gabe. "Next time I tear the arm out of its goddamn socket."

"But I'm telling the—"

Gabe started to push and the man cried out.

"Wait! I'll talk!"

"I already know what you're supposed to tell me," said Gabe. "But I want the truth and I'll kill you if I don't get it."

The man groaned, the side of his face pressed against the carriage house floor. Blood poured into his eyes and dripped into the dirt. He struggled against Gabe's hold but he couldn't get the leverage he needed. Then he felt more pressure on his arm and settled down. Gabe pulled one of his Remingtons and pressed the muzzle hard into the man's ear.

"Talk now or I pull the trigger," he said. "Makes no difference to me."

Gabe's tone was casual and the man believed it. "Shit," he said, "it's not like I know anything. There was someone in a saloon handing out money."

"For what?"

The man hesitated and Gabe rolled the hammer back.

"Shit!" the man said again. "We had to burn the house and kill 'em all."

Gabe shuddered, yearning to pull the trigger. "Who hired you?"

"I told you, the guy in the saloon."

"Was he there tonight?"

"He was across from me, behind the tree."

"He's still there."

"Then you got him, huh?"

"Except it wasn't his money," said Gabe, bearing down on the revolver. "And you know that, right? *Who hired you?*"

"I never heard any names, damn it! All I know is that someone else supplied the weapons. I think he has a hardware store."

"Good enough," said Gabe. "You'll tell that to a judge?"

"Shit, he wouldn't believe me."

"Then I get to kill you right here," said Gabe. There was no mistaking the anticipation in his voice.

"I'll *talk*, all right? Jesus Christ!" The man was staring up at him from the corner of one white eye. "It's just that I don't know that much."

"What about the man with the hardware store? Were you supposed to meet him afterwards?"

"Shit, he wouldn't get within a thousand miles of us."

Gabe scowled, knowing it had to be true. He slipped the Remington back into its holster. "You wouldn't get all your payment in advance," he said. "How were you supposed to get the rest?"

"That other guy. The one you killed."

"How much?" said Gabe. "What's it worth to murder four good people?"

"Five hundred dollars. And the woman."

Gabe caught his breath. "What woman?"

"Kind of a bonus, I guess. There was gonna be a woman we could all take turns with. Do whatever we wanted."

"Where?"

The eye studied him with a crafty look. "You're worried about her, ain't you?"

"Where!"

The man laughed into the dirt. "I figure that's worth something, mister. Let me go if I tell you?"

Gabe wrenched the man's arm in both hands and heard a loud, hard pop from his shoulder. The killer screamed and bucked in a wild frenzy but Gabe rode him down, taking hold of the other wrist.

"It's worth one good arm," Gabe told him. "Have we got a deal?"

The man nodded and Gabe let him up. He was still whimpering, hugging his useless arm against his side and wincing at the slightest movement. They walked back through the alley in a silvery dawn light, birds singing from bushes and rooftops all around them. It seemed strange to hear such happy sounds while the man described the street and house he was supposed to look for after the fire and the killings.

They found it quickly and went through a rusty iron gate. From the porch Gabe glanced down the street, squinting at a small figure hurrying away in the distance. Then he shrugged and opened a door with an oval window of frosted glass, raising an eyebrow at the killer.

"Down below," the man said in a defeated tone. "There's a cellar, I guess."

He looked a little more lively when they went down the stairs from the kitchen and found Sarah on her back on the mattress, arms and legs spread out at her sides. She started crying as soon as she saw Gabe.

"Oh, thank God!" she said, her voice ragged but full of relief.

Gabe wore a dark, brooding look as he kneeled to untie the knots at Sarah's ankles. He was remembering Jane Tomlin in the line shack. "Seems like this happens to women who get mixed up with Chester. Sorry I got you into this, Sarah."

"You!" she said. "*I'm* the one that took the money, remember? *I* made the choice."

Gabe heard a soft moan and looked over his shoulder to find the killer staring down at the woman. Blood and dirt were caked on his face and he still hugged his dangling arm to his side, but all of that had been forgotten in a kind of rapture that made his eyes glassy.

"What's your name?" Gabe asked him.

The killer blinked. "Gorman," he said. "Jeff Gorman."

"Well, Gorman, do you want to shake hands with me? Good and hard?"

"No!" said the man. He stepped back, looking frightened and confused.

"Then turn the fuck around!"

Gorman jumped, obeying reluctantly while Gabe went back to work on the knots at Sarah's wrists.

"Who's that?" she said. "One of the men Tomlin hired?"

Gabe nodded.

"He looks terrible."

"He deserves worse," said Gabe. "What the hell are these?" He was staring at bruises that covered Sarah's breasts and arms and the inside of her thighs. Some were blue-black, others a yellowish green. "That son of a bitch!" he said. "I hope I get a chance to kill him myself."

"They'll heal," Sarah said grimly. "But I want payment from the bastard. I want the five thousand dollars he promised."

"He never gave it to you?"

"He gave it to me, all right. Then he took it out of my bag before he left."

"Was that just now?" said Gabe, getting excited. "I thought I saw him."

Sarah nodded and Gabe's excitement grew. He helped the woman to her feet and picked her dress off the floor.

"We can catch him," he was saying. "We can take the money back." Then he saw where Tomlin had torn Sarah's dress and his shoulders sagged. "There goes that idea. You can't appear like this in public."

"Maybe I could put your shirt over it?" said Sarah. "Just long enough to get back to my place."

Gabe shrugged and said, "Of course. But that means we lose Tomlin."

"He's on his way home! He has to change clothes and then he'll stop for breakfast before he goes to court. What do you bet he doesn't want to carry the money around with him?"

"So it'll be somewhere in the house."

"And he won't."

Gabe nodded, trying to keep the disappointment out of his eyes. "Then you decided against testifying?" he said. "Not that we really need it, I guess—"

"Gabe."

"We still have our friend Gorman, here. And there's a deputy who'll talk about the sheriff."

Sarah was laughing. "Gabe, will you shut up! The sooner we find that money the sooner you can get me to the hearing."

"You mean you're still willing? Even after seeing how much power he has?"

"He bought that power," Sarah said scornfully. "Without Jane's money he'll be nothing more than what he looks like."

Gabe laughed. "That ain't much," he said.

"I can hardly wait."

A doctor named Lowery cleaned and patched the bullet hole in Nate Brandon's leg, then applied some ointment to a patch of burn blisters on Jane Tomlin's arm. Lowery left the marshal's office a little after seven, meeting the county attorney on his way in. The attorney's name was Dyson and he was still there half an hour later when a volunteer standing by the front window straightened up a little and said, "Mr. McClure?"

The marshal went to look over the man's shoulder, then opened the door and stepped out into the street. Harry Thorne met him in front of the boardwalk, holding a shotgun across his waist. Seven other men formed a tight semi-circle behind the sheriff. McClure peered at them one at a time, his grey eyes flat and mild. Then he turned back to Thorne, tilting his head back a little to meet the big man's eyes.

"What's the occasion?" said the marshal. "Looks like you've called out every deputy in Cheyenne County."

"Someone has to keep order in this town," said Thorne. "You sure as hell ain't doin' it."

"It's been hard," the older man admitted.

"Now I hear there was an attack on Jane Tomlin and Frank Haywood."

"It's not exactly a secret, Harry. Everyone in town has known about it for two hours."

"Very funny," said Thorne, a powerful hatred burning deep in his eyes. "What folks don't seem to know is whether the two of 'em survived."

"Good," said McClure. "That's the way I wanted it."

"Did they?"

"Why?"

"Because I've come to get 'em if they did," said Thorne. "The woman needs protection and Haywood's still my prisoner."

McClure rocked back on his heels, watching the sheriff with an idle, placid expression. After a few seconds it was obvious that he didn't plan to answer.

"Goddamn it," said Thorne, "hand 'em over right now or I'll go in and find 'em. It's up to you, McClure."

The marshal heard steps on the boardwalk and knew his deputies were coming out with the volunteers, fanning out to the left and right behind him. Thorne watched them with a steadily deepening frown.

"This ain't right," he said. "A lot of people are gonna get hurt."

"Glad to hear you say it," McClure told him. "Does it mean you'll give yourself up?"

"What the hell does *that* mean?"

"Steve Shlisky's in my office, Harry."

Thorne studied McClure with an uncertain look, but all he saw were the marshal's blank expression and a weariness in his eyes. "Good!" said the sheriff. "I want him too. I think he knows what happened to Frank."

"He does, Harry. That's why Andrew Dyson is in there with him, taking his deposition."

"Deposition!" said Thorne. "The county attorney?" He reared his head back and glared at the marshal. "What the hell are you tryin' to pull, McClure? What are you gettin' him to say?"

The marshal shook his head. "It won't work, Harry. Steve knows you were down there when Frank was getting strangled. He's swearin' to it right now."

"He's lying!" the sheriff roared. "He's tryin' to save his own skin and you're helpin' him, just to get at me."

"Can't you tell when you're licked!" said McClure, deciding to add some extra pressure. "Steve's just backing up the story we already have, you know. Frank woke up just before you hit him. He saw you do it, Harry."

"He's lying too! You're ganging up on me and I'm gonna arrest every last one of you."

McClure was shaking his head again. "No you're not, Harry. I wired the governor at five-thirty this morning and he's ordered you out of office."

"Horseshit!" said Thorne. "He can't do that."

McClure pulled a small square of yellow paper from his pocket and handed it across, watching the change in the sheriff's expression as he read the telegram. McClure was thinking about how hard it would be to lose your job and learn you were being accused of attempted murder, all at once and all in front of the men who'd been working for you. It would be even worse to suffer the defeat at the hands of an old enemy. McClure understood the trapped, hounded look in Thorne's eyes. He even felt a little sorry for the man. But he also felt a lot of satisfaction that Thorne was finally getting what he deserved. It might have made McClure's tone a little smug.

"It's all there," he said as the sheriff read. "The governor wants me to appoint one of your deputies as an acting sheriff. And of course I have to take you into custody."

Thorne let the telegram fall into the dirt, grinding it beneath his heel as he gripped the shotgun in both hands again. He stared at the marshal with a hot, challenging look and said, "That's what I think of the goddamn governor."

There was a trace of pity in McClure's laughter. "And that's about what he can do to *you*, Harry. Admit it, you were a fool to throw in with Chester Tomlin. Don't add stupidity to foolishness."

"You son of a bitch!" said Thorne. He swung the butt of his shotgun, something that felt to him like a sudden impulse. But the older man had seen it coming for a long time. His hands flashed in the morning sun and he grabbed the shotgun before it touched his head.

There was a dry rattle of cocking hammers from the porch and an answering rattle from the sheriff's deputies in the street. But McClure was spinning out of the way, pulling the shotgun up and over his shoulder. He pulled the sheriff along with it. Thorne's body twisted off-balance and his feet tangled and he fell, slamming a shoulder into the hard-packed dirt in the street. He grunted as the wind was knocked out of him. He also loosened his grip on the shotgun for an instant, and McClure was waiting to wrench it out of his hands.

"Stay out of this," he ordered the men on the boardwalk. Then he threw a hard look at the county deputies and said, "You too, understand? This is just between him and me."

Thorne was struggling to his feet. "Big talk," he said disdainfully. "Especially for a man with a gun in his hands."

"You're still missing the point," McClure said with equal scorn. "Who gives a shit whether you can whip me or I can whip you? Now you'd better *think*, Harry. You have to *act smart*."

The sheriff made a grab for his weapon but McClure

dropped it low and used it like a battering ram. The big double bore buried itself several inches deep in Thorne's belly and he doubled over, gasping as he stumbled backwards. Then he came at the sheriff again with a wild glitter of rage in his eyes. McClure swung the shotgun up and over the sheriff's outstretched hands, slamming the barrel into his skull just above the ear. There was a sharp crack that echoed across the street as the big man dropped to his knees. He was holding his head and blood was oozing out between his fingers.

"Had enough?" said McClure.

But Thorne lunged from a kneeling position, grabbing the marshal's legs and trying to drag him to the ground. McClure steadied himself and smashed down with the stock of the shotgun, hitting just above the sheriff's kidney. Thorne cried out and rolled onto his back. McClure kneeled beside him and pressed the barrel of the weapon across his throat.

"Now by God you're gonna listen to me!" he yelled. "Do you hear?"

Thorne nodded weakly, trying to twist his massive neck out from under the steel barrel.

"I keep tryin' to tell you you're licked," said the marshal, "and you keep gettin' mad at me. But it's Chester Tomlin who done this to you. Haven't you figured that out yet?"

The sheriff was eyeing him with the familiar hatred and bitterness, but also with a look of dawning comprehension. McClure eased the pressure on the shotgun.

"If you gotta blame somebody besides yourself," said the marshal, "blame *Tomlin*. What did he do, promise you a lot of money? Did he promise to get the ranch back for you?"

Thorne didn't say anything.

"I thought so," said McClure. "You were a fool to listen

to the man, Harry, *but he knew your weak spot*. He knew what you wanted and he played you like a goddamn fish, just to get what *he* wanted.''

The bitterness in the sheriff's eyes had shifted in some way. He wasn't looking at McClure so much as through him. The marshal released the shotgun and got to his feet.

''There's only one thing you can do,'' he said. ''It'll make things go easier for you at the trial, and you'll have a chance to get back at the bastard who used you.''

Thorne was struggling to his feet. He heard steps on the boardwalk and looked up, then quickly looked away. Frank Haywood and Jane Tomlin had come through the door. They stood above the steps while the silence stretched on.

''It's almost time for the hearing,'' McClure finally said. ''What do you say, Harry? Will you talk to Wilcox?''

''Yeah,'' Thorne grunted. ''I'll talk.''

''Give me your badge, then.''

Thorne pulled it off his vest and held it out, his eyes still fixed on the ground. The marshal took it from him and squinted at the county lawmen, some of whom looked as if they were still trying to make up their minds.

''Hrachovec,'' McClure said to one of them, ''you want the job until we can hold another election?''

The deputy offered a shy smile and said, ''Sure! With a vote of confidence like that I might even run for sheriff myself.''

''Good,'' said McClure. ''Any objections from the rest of you?''

The other deputies looked at each other and a couple of them shrugged.

''Good,'' McClure said again. ''Get back to your jobs and let's forget about this morning, all right?'' The deputies started drifting away as the marshal turned back to the former sheriff. "Come on inside, Thorne. We'll get that head patched up before the hearing."

A few minutes later Thorne was at the center of a small procession moving toward the county courthouse. McClure was at his side, with the rancher and Jane Tomlin behind them. They were flanked by four of McClure's deputies who were acting as guards, while Haywood's four friends had tagged along to see how things turned out.

They were joined by a smaller procession at a street corner two blocks from the courthouse. Gabe Conrad was leading a black-haired man who wore a sullen look of suffering as he hugged his arm to his side. Sarah Prater marched along ahead of Gabe, swinging her purse and grinning, looking as happy as the outlaw looked miserable. McClure studied her with a puzzled frown as the two groups merged. Then he glanced at the outlaw before his eyes finally came to rest on Gabe.

"This the fella behind the fence?" he asked.

Gabe looked surprised. Then he laughed. "Why do I keep underestimating you," he said.

McClure grinned. "No one expects much from an old man," he said. "But it don't take much to see an abandoned carbine and a splotch of blood in the grass."

"You did say we should leave one alive, Marshal. His name's Jeff Gorman and he was recruited in a saloon. The tough who gave him the money told him to say it was Frank Haywood that did the recruiting—if anyone asked."

McClure nodded and said, "That'll help a lot, Gabe. It fits right in with the things our former sheriff will have to say."

"Just wait till the judge hears *my* story," Sarah put in.

Frank Haywood was looking grim. "Then there's Mrs. Tomlin and me," he said. "We won't exactly be silent."

"I'm beginning to wonder if anyone will *have* to testify,"

said McClure. "Chester might fold as soon as he sees who's coming into the courtroom."

"We've sure got the cards," Gabe agreed, beginning to feel the excitement of finally beating the storekeeper. Then he laughed, and saw that the others gave him quizzical looks. "Five witnesses," he explained. "Our five aces in the hole. That's the best damn poker hand I've ever seen!"

CHAPTER SIXTEEN

Gabe tried to imagine how they must have looked as they crowded into the courtroom, thirteen men and two women who had been awake for all or most of the night. One of them wore a floor-length coat made from an old piece of buffalo hide, with a Lakota symbol painted on the back. Two others still wore clothes that were torn and streaked with soot from the fire. Neither of the women had had the time for cosmetics or even for combing her hair, and a clean white bandage covered the length of Jane Tomlin's arm. Another bandage was wrapped around Harry Thorne's head, while Jeff Gorman's black hair was caked with blood and his face streaked with dirt.

Judge Roland Wilcox was already waiting behind the bench when they came in, his bushy white eyebrows furrowed in an impatient frown that grew deeper as he watched the intrusion.

"What the hell is going on?" he demanded, glaring at

McClure. "This is supposed to be a court hearing, not a circus."

Then Wilcox started getting a chance to see the marshal's companions. McClure had arranged his deputies and volunteers in a tight circle around the witnesses, but now they were all taking seats in the front of the room. The judge's face went through a comical series of changes as he recognized individual members of the crowd and noticed their condition.

That's when Gabe started keeping an eye on Chester Tomlin, who was sitting by himself in the back. The changes in his expression were a lot more rewarding. They started with vaguely nervous curiosity, until he saw the black-haired outlaw named Gorman. That made Tomlin look worried even though he'd never actually seen the man before. Two more deputies sat down and the storekeeper saw his wife next to Frank Haywood. His face filled with alarm, and then went pale when he saw Sarah Prater.

But even that was mild compared to the effect of seeing Harry Thorne with an empty holster and nothing but a couple of holes in his vest where his badge had been. Thorne caught sight of Tomlin about the same time and gave him a hard, level-lidded stare.

The storekeeper jumped up and ran out of the courtroom.

Gabe glanced at McClure, who was getting ready to address Judge Wilcox. The marshal dipped his chin before he turned toward the bench.

"Your honor," McClure began, "Mr. Dyson's on his way. But let me call your attention to a few developments . . ."

That was all Gabe heard before the courtroom door closed behind him. He was already on the stairs, listening to the hollow echo of footsteps several landings below. By the time

he got outside Tomlin was running up the middle of the wide
street. The storekeeper glanced over his shoulder and ran
even harder. His arms pumped frantically up and down and
his feet churned the dirt, leaving little puffs of orange dust in
the clear morning air.

Gabe followed only fast enough to keep pace, closing the
gap when Tomlin stopped to fumble with a ring of keys in
front of his hardware store. He threw the door open and went
inside. When Gabe followed him in a few seconds later,
Tomlin was behind the same display case that had separated
them the first day they met. Now there was another Winchester in the storekeeper's arms and he was pressing a single
shell into its loading port. He worked the lever and tried to
point the rifle at Gabe.

But all of this had given Gabe plenty of time to slip the
Remington out of his shoulder holster and take careful aim
with the one remaining ball in the spare cylinder. It smashed
Tomlin's shoulder and he spun away while the carbine
crashed to the floor.

Gabe put up the empty gun but Tomlin stayed on his feet,
bending to pick up the rifle again in his good hand. Gabe
scowled and took the second Remington off his hip, aware
that it contained only two good loads. Then he realized that
Tomlin hadn't turned back to face him. Instead the storekeeper was trying to tuck the muzzle of the Winchester under
his chin.

"Oh no you don't," said Gabe, grimly putting a ball
through Tomlin's other shoulder.

The carbine dropped to the floor again and Tomlin
screamed, rushing Gabe with his head down as if he was
trying to clear a path to the door. Gabe clubbed the
storekeeper with his revolver and Tomlin went sprawling,
landing on one of the wounded shoulders.

"Dear God," he cried out. "Just kill me and get it over with!"

Gabe shook his head. "That would be too easy, Tomlin."

"You know you want to."

"Maybe. But that's always been your stock in trade, hasn't it? If you know what people want then you're in the saddle."

"You got me wrong—"

"I finally got you *right,* you bastard. You still don't give a damn how much suffering you've caused. But now I have a chance to make sure you do a little suffering of your own. You're gonna stick around long enough to watch everything *you* wanted go down the drain."

"Please—"

"Your money and all your property," said Gabe, a cruel light shining in his eyes. "Not to mention your wife. And the respect of the people in town. It'll all get stripped away, Tomlin. You won't have a damn thing left."

"Please!" the storekeeper whimpered. "I'm begging you to kill me."

"Keep begging," said Gabe. "I'm enjoying it."

Tomlin tried to sit up but Gabe put one foot on his chest and gave him a violent push. A moment later there was a clatter on the boardwalk outside and then Sam McClure was coming through the door, followed by Sarah Prater, Frank Haywood and Jane Tomlin. Sarah came over to Gabe and squeezed herself against him, shuddering when she looked down at Chester Tomlin.

"It was easy," the marshal told Gabe. "I didn't have to say very much at all before Wilcox was ready to let Frank go. Dyson is still over there, filling in the rest of the story. He'll get indictments for Mr. Thorne and Mr. Tomlin"— McClure was staring down at the blood splashed across the storekeeper's coat—"assuming he lives long enough, of course."

"He'll be around for the trial," Gabe assured him. "I made sure of that. He'll also be around for the wedding between his ex-wife and Frank Haywood."

The rancher laughed and put his arm around Jane Tomlin's shoulders while the storekeeper stared up at them, looking as miserable as his wife looked joyful. Gabe very nearly pitied the man. Sweat was popping out on his face as the pain of his wounds took hold, mingling with the anguish of his defeat. The storekeeper closed his eyes and rolled onto his side, curling his knees up against his arms. Gabe found himself remembering the first day he came into the store. He sighed deeply and looked at the rancher.

"I have to admit it," he said. "You were right and I was wrong."

Haywood gave him a puzzled frown. "About what?"

"We were standing right here, remember? You told me I was making a mistake."

Haywood's frown slowly disappeared as the memory returned. "That's right!" he said with an explosive laugh. "You'd just finished whippin' me, by God. No one ever done it before."

"That doesn't change the fact I made a mistake," Gabe said ruefully. "I stepped in on the wrong side, from the very beginning."

Haywood hugged Jane Tomlin a little closer. "Mostly you were on her side," he said. "That's what counts."

The storekeeper was rocking back and forth on the floor and moaning softly, like a small boy trying not to hear anything.

"Besides," Haywood added with another laugh, "you said that was your first mistake in ten years, right?"

Gabe grinned, shrugging his shoulders. "Maybe I forgot a couple."

The rancher turned serious. "I doubt it," he said, looking from Gabe to Sam McClure. "Let's go somewhere and celebrate, and I'll make a toast to the two best men I've ever known."

SONS OF TEXAS

**Book one in the exciting new saga
of America's Lone Star state!**

TOM EARLY

Texas, 1816. A golden land of
opportunity for anyone who dared
to stake a claim in its destiny...and
its dangers...

Filled with action, adventure,
drama and romance, *Sons of Texas*
is the magnificent epic story of
America in the making...the
people, places, and passions that
made our country great.

Look for each new book in the series!